pish posh

pish posh

ELLEN POTTER

SCHOLASTIC INC.

New York Toronto London Auckland Sydney
Mexico City New Delhi Hong Kong Buenos Aires

ISBN-13: 978-0-439-89786-0
ISBN-10: 0-439-89786-6

12 11 10 9 8 7 6 5 4 3 2 1   6 7 8 9 10 11/0

Printed in the U.S.A.   40

First Scholastic printing, September 2006

Design by Gina DiMassi

Text set in Administer

For Ron Campbell and Todd Herron,
my glittery and fabulous friends

Acknowledgments:

My heartfelt thanks to the following bona fide Somebodies
(even Ms. Mandy says these folks are the real deal):
Michael Green, my editor; my agent, Alice Tasman;
my husband, Adam; and Jessica Dougherty,
one of the wisest thirteen-year-olds on the planet.

CHAPTER ONE

If you walked into the Pish Posh restaurant on any given night, you would be sure to find a smallish eleven-year-old girl wearing large black sunglasses sitting by herself at a little round table in the back. She had excellent posture and kept quite still—no fidgeting, no hair twisting, no smiling—while she watched the glittery and fabulous customers come and go. Because her glasses were so large and so black, you could not tell whom she was looking at, which made the glittery, fabulous customers at the Pish Posh restaurant very, very nervous.

Today, the girl in the dark glasses, whose name was Clara Frankofile, was sitting at her customary table with a tuna-fish sandwich, cut into four perfect triangles, and a tall glass of tomato juice with a straw. She had not touched the sandwich, but she took regular and small sips from the tomato juice as she gazed around the restaurant with sharp, assessing eyes.

It was the middle of August and New York City was experiencing a heat wave, but Clara was not dressed in shorts and a T-shirt, like most eleven-year-old girls. Instead, she wore a simple black dress. It was the same dress that she wore every day (well, not the same, exact one—she owned 157 copies of it). In fact, she had been wearing the same simple black dress, in varying sizes, since the day she was born. Her parents, who owned the Pish Posh restaurant, had decided that a simple black dress was the epitome of style, and that their child should always look stylish. They had a tailor sew tiny, simple black dresses no bigger than a napkin for the infant Clara. And as she grew, they found no reason for their daughter to stop wearing simple black dresses. When she was eight years old, Clara decided to add a pair of large black sunglasses to her outfit, and tucked away in her jewelry box was a necklace strung with perfect Tahitian pearls, which she intended to start wearing when she turned sixteen.

True, the other kids at school teased her for wearing the same thing every day, but Clara paid no attention to them. Her classmates, she had discovered, were all astonishingly stupid. She had changed schools many times, hoping to find children who were as intelligent and elegant as she was. But, amazingly, each school seemed to be filled with children who were even stupider and more vulgar than the children at the previous school.

At a table in the center of the restaurant, a dashing and very popular movie star with sunny blond highlights in his hair eyed Clara nervously.

"Is she looking our way?" he asked the woman sitting across from him. She was equally blonde, with bunchy pink lips, like a wad of already-chewed bubble gum.

"I don't think so, darling," the woman said.

"She is! I can feel her eyes on me! I told you I shouldn't have put those highlights in my hair. I can't eat a bite, not a bite!"

"No, my poor darling. She is looking at that horrible woman at the corner table—yes, the very thin one with a face like a catfish. She's a ballerina, darling, and she fell flat on her behind last night during a performance! People are saying that her career is finished, darling, but absolutely! Now eat your salmon tartare . . . and then perhaps we can visit the hairdresser and do something about those awful highlights! What on earth were you thinking?"

But Clara was not looking at the movie star or the ballerina at all. Nor was she looking at the princess of Thailand, who had the most atrocious table manners and was rolling up bits of baguette between her fingers and lobbing them at her bodyguards.

In fact, Clara Frankofile was staring most intently at a plain little man in a crisp gray suit and neatly combed white hair. He sat by himself, eating sautéed chicken livers, his hand shaking ever so slightly as he lifted the fork to his lips. To the average human, there would be nothing at all interesting about this man. But behind her glasses, Clara's sharp green eyes followed his smallest movements.

"Another tomato juice, baby doll?"

Clara's concentration was broken by the new waiter, a young man with a mass of black curly hair. He smiled at her, and his teeth were so bright and white, they seemed to mock her. "You're sipping spit, baby doll." He pointed to her glass, which was indeed practically empty.

"What is your name?" Clara demanded.

"Tom."

"Well, Tom, I realize that you are new at Pish Posh." Clara deliberately kept the anger out of her voice. Her father had told her that it was best not to let the workers see that you had any emotion. "But if you ever call me baby doll again, or say the word *spit* in front of me, I will have you fired immediately."

The young man smiled again, this time a little less brightly.

"Would the young lady care for more tomato juice?" Tom asked. He was using the right words, but Clara had the gnawing feeling that he was not taking her seriously.

"No. Take that away." She nodded toward her glass. "And don't speak to me anymore." Then she turned away from him and fixed her sights back on the little man with white hair. When a tapioca pudding was delivered to his table for dessert, Clara smiled for the first time that night—a small, exceedingly tight smile.

Then she rose from the table. The whole restaurant grew silent, and all eyes turned to watch her as she walked, straight-backed as a soldier, to the front of the restaurant. There were low murmurs as she passed. Everyone was wide-eyed and jittery, and no one seemed to breathe.

"Mother," Clara said to a tall, willowy woman, who was the restaurant's hostess.

The woman was dressed in a sweeping red gown, and her hair was wrapped in a white, jewel-encrusted turban, which looked a little bit like a giant diaper. She appeared not to have heard Clara, as she was hovering over a thick leather book, opened to a page listing all the people who had reservations at Pish Posh for that evening.

"Mother," Clara repeated more forcefully, and she poked her mother's waist—just a small poke. But she knew everyone was watching her, and she hated to be ignored. Her mother looked at her waist for a moment, as if she had a sudden cramp, and then noticed her daughter.

"What is it, Clara?"

"Mother, it's Dr. Piff. We must ask him to leave and never return." This made Lila Frankofile turn and look at her daughter and then at the little man in the gray suit.

"Dr. Piff? But why?"

"He has become a Nobody."

"Are you sure, Clara?"

"I am *quite* sure," Clara replied smartly, offended that her mother would even question her judgment.

"Oh." Lila patted her turban sadly. "What a pity. He's been eating at Pish Posh every night since we opened. As I remember, you used to be quite fond of him, when you were a little girl." Lila sighed. "But I suppose it can't be helped."

Lila closed the reservation book, adjusted her turban, and strode over to Dr. Piff's table. The entire restaurant let out their breath all at once as they watched Lila Frankofile approach Dr. Piff's table. Across the room, murmurs of relief could be heard: "Thank heavens!" and "I thought for sure it was going to be me!"

Her work having been done, Clara Frankofile strode back to her table. She sat down and for the first time that evening

5

took a small bite out of her sandwich. It was made just the way she liked it—with paper-thin slices of tomato on sourdough bread. She had just finished the first triangle and had begun on the second when Dr. Piff came up to her table.

"May I sit down?" he asked.

This had never happened before. No one had ever asked to sit down at her table, much less someone who had just been identified as a Nobody. For a moment Clara felt paralyzed, and she stared at him rather stupidly. But then she collected herself and replied in what she hoped was an indifferent tone, "If you must."

He sat down in his quiet way and smoothed his white hair with the palm of his hand.

"How did you know, may I ask?" he said.

"How did I know that you have become a Nobody, do you mean?" Now Clara sat up a little straighter. This was a topic she enjoyed, because she prided herself on being able to root out a Nobody in a roomful of Somebodies, even if the person had only just recently become a Nobody.

"It wasn't difficult, after all—not if you really paid attention. Most people don't, however," Clara explained. "First, I noticed your shoes when you came in. They were dull and scuffed. The very first thing that a brand-new Nobody does is neglect his footwear. Then I noticed that you ordered the tapioca pudding, which is a dessert that people order when they are feeling nostalgic about their childhood. And important people get nostalgic about their childhood only when they are no longer important. But most of all"—Clara took a breath and lifted her chin—"I noticed that your right hand was trembling. Just a tiny bit. But you are an eye surgeon, Dr. Piff, and an eye surgeon *cannot* have a shaky hand."

"Very clever, Clara." Dr. Piff nodded appreciatively. "And you are absolutely correct."

"I'm sorry, Dr. Piff," Clara said, and she looked away. She wished he would leave her alone with her tuna-fish sandwich.

Then Dr. Piff did the most extraordinary thing. He reached across the table and removed her sunglasses. Clara gasped and her back stiffened.

"What did you do that for?" she demanded angrily.

"I used to take you skating in Central Park on Sundays," he said, absently holding the glasses between his fingers. Clara began to wonder if he had gone mad. She glanced around the restaurant to see if she could summon one of the busboys to help her, but no one was nearby.

"You were such an enchanting child," he continued. "You used to whistle while you skated. You said it helped you keep your balance."

"I don't remember that at all, Dr. Piff. Please give me back my glasses."

Dr. Piff looked very seriously into Clara's eyes. No one had ever looked so seriously and closely at her eyes before. It made her feel very small and breakable. Then Dr. Piff sighed and handed her the glasses, which she promptly put back on.

"You have a very cunning pair of eyes, Clara." He had lowered his voice to almost a whisper. "But surely you can't know *everything* that happens at Pish Posh."

"Of course I do!" she said indignantly. "I know every-thing that happens in this restaurant! You don't believe me? Look over there." She pointed to Fiona Babbish, the pale, sickly, rather tragic-looking young heiress, who always dined alone at a table near the back. "Do you see that fly on the edge of her bowl of squid chowder? That fly came in through the front door at seven twenty-eight P.M., hovered around my mother's head for seven seconds, then flew close to the princess of Thailand's baguette, where her bodyguard tried to catch it in his hand, but missed. Now Fiona Babbish will stare at it sadly for a few seconds—look at her lower lip droop—decide that it has ruined her entire dinner—look at her eyes well up with tears—and will stand up and leave . . . *now.*" At which point Fiona Babbish stood on her thin, fee-ble legs, adjusted her pink Chanel suit, and minced out of the restaurant.

"And yet," continued Dr. Piff, as if he hadn't heard her, still in a quiet voice, "you have failed to notice a most pe-culiar and mysterious thing that is happening right under your nose."

"Nonsense!" Clara declared. "If there was anything at all peculiar *or* mysterious happening here, I would be the first to know about it."

Dr. Piff smiled a little and shrugged. "Perhaps it is better that you haven't noticed. It would probably unnerve such an elegant young lady as yourself. Well, Clara"—Dr. Piff stood up and put on his gray hat, then tipped it at her—"I wish you a good evening and a life free of troubles."

With that, he walked out of Pish Posh for the last time.

CHAPTER TWO

Clara sat at her table a moment longer, staring absently at the remaining three triangles of tuna-fish sandwich. The conversation with Dr. Piff had upset her. What in the world had he meant? *Peculiar and mysterious?* How could there be something at Pish Posh that she had failed to notice? She decided Dr. Piff was mistaken. Or perhaps he was just a liar. She thought about what he'd told her—that she used to whistle to keep her balance while she ice-skated. That was simply not true. She never, ever whistled. Whistling was for people who had unimportant lives. Her maid whistled, for instance. She determined then and there that Dr. Piff was a chronic liar and that she would think no more about it. But still, when she picked up her sandwich to take a bite, she found that she had lost her appetite.

The customers in the restaurant were no longer watching her. In fact, they had forgotten all about her, since she had clearly chosen the Nobody and they were safe. Her eyes drifted over to the princess of Thailand, who was only two years older than she was. The princess had stopped throwing bits of baguette, and now she had engaged one of her body-guards in a sword fight, using their utensils. She was laughing loudly, and all the bodyguards were laughing, too. She was acting just like the girls at Clara's school, which was very unbecoming of a princess. In a fit of pique, Clara thought that she would have the princess declared a Nobody. *That* would stop her laughing! But then, she knew that was impossible. That was the problem with royalty—they almost never became Nobodies, even when they acted like savages.

Clara rose and walked up to her mother.

"I'm going home," Clara said.

"So soon?"

Just then, Prim LeDander and her friend Bitsey Fopah walked through the door. They were both terribly thin, terribly rich, and, amazingly, without eyebrows.

"Hello, ladies, and how are—" Lila started, but when she noticed the pale, smooth skin where their eyebrows should have been, she stopped.

"Are you looking at our eyebrows, darling?" Prim asked.

"Not at all." Lila quickly collected herself. "Why on earth should I look at your eyebrows?"

"We've had them waxed," Prim said in a quiet, confidential voice.

"It was dreadfully painful," moaned Bitsey.

"It's all the rage," said Prim. "On account of the upcoming medieval costume exhibit at the Metropolitan Museum."

"The women were born without eyebrows back in the Middle Ages, you see," Bitsey explained, and she raised the skin where her eyebrows should have been to show just how shocking this piece of information was.

"Nonsense, Bitsey! They simply plucked them all out." Prim turned to Lila. "It makes the eyes look wider, you see." She opened her eyes wide to demonstrate.

"Extraordinary!" Lila exclaimed.

"The museum is going to choose the 'Face of the Middle Ages' among New York's high society—" Bitsey said.

"Of which we are most certainly the highest," Prim added.

"—and whomever they choose will have her face cast in a mold, out of which they will create the mannequins that wear the costumes in the exhibit. Can you imagine! Your own face being on permanent display in the Metropolitan Museum of Art! Oh, wouldn't that make one's friends revoltingly jealous!"

"Deliciously so!" Prim agreed.

Clara went into the kitchen to say good night to her father, Pierre Frankofile. He was the owner of Pish Posh, but he was also the chef. Right now, he stood behind the shelves of gleaming metal where they put the plates of food, and was sautéing onions in a black-singed pan. He wore a white chef's jacket and a white chef's hat, and his round face was sweaty and pink.

"I'm going home, Papa," said Clara. She had to speak very loudly over the clatter of pots and pans and the roar of the dishwasher and the yells of the waiters calling their orders. The kitchen had at least ten other people working in it, chopping garlic, grilling meat, stirring soup, and in the back, washing racks of dishes and glasses in a giant silver dishwasher. Clara did not like the kitchen. It was dirty and hot and chaotic, and the workers were, of course, not the sort she cared to have anything to do with. In fact, she only ever came into the kitchen to say good night to her father.

Pierre Frankofile turned away from his pan of onions to say good night to his daughter, when his eyes suddenly shifted to the woman ladling up the soup.

"Audrey, you *imbécile!* You have garnished the soup with a carrot peel instead of parsley! Can you not tell the difference?!" He spoke with a slight French accent, having grown up in a luxurious chateau in France, with a slew of nannies and governesses, before moving to the United States as a teenager.

"I'm sorry, Chef Frankofile," Audrey, the soup-maker, said. She was a tall, slender young woman with a mass of bright red hair pulled back into a tight ponytail. Her thick glasses were steamed up at the moment from the squid chowder simmering in the pot.

"Well, have your eyes examined, you blind bat, or I will slice off your right thumb and serve it up as shish kebob, is that understood?!" Mr. Frankofile's face was perfectly red now and his eyes were bulging. Yet no one else in the kitchen even bothered to look up from what they were doing, since he yelled at them and called them nasty things on a regular basis.

"Well, good night, Papa," Clara said.

"*Oui, bon soir,* Cla—hey you! The new dishwasher! Yes, you, the boneheaded moron!" A perspiring, tattooed young man had just pulled a tray full of water glasses out of the steamy dishwasher. "If you break one of those glasses, I will hang you upside down from your—" Clara missed the rest of her father's tirade as she walked out the back door.

Outside, the evening was warm, but there was an occasional cool breeze that felt wonderful on Clara's shoulders. Across the street was Washington Square Park, a busy, loud park with a great marble arch at its entranceway. Her father had told her that he bought the restaurant because it faced the arch, which reminded him of the Arc de Triomphe in Paris.

The streets were busy, full of people chatting and laughing on their way to somewhere else—the theater, a party. They were people who would never be allowed in Pish Posh— not in a million years—and it amazed her that they could still be so cheerful.

On her walk home she thought again of what Dr. Piff had said. What on earth was he talking about? Her mind sifted through all the possibilities, but she could come up with nothing and, frustrated, she resolved not to think about it again.

At least not until tomorrow.

The Frankofiles lived in a high-rise luxury apartment building, just a few blocks uptown from Pish Posh. They owned the top two floors, so that Lila and Pierre lived on the thirty-fourth floor and Clara lived on the thirty-fifth floor. This way, Lila and Pierre explained to their friends, no one got in anyone else's way.

"Hello?" Clara called when she entered her apartment. Sometimes the maid was still there in the early evening. She listened for whistling, but the apartment was perfectly silent.

To take her mind off Dr. Piff, she thought she should try to amuse herself. She ambled past the grand living room with its sumptuous Moroccan carpets and its green silk couches and armchairs and, hanging above it all, a great chandelier with a hundred crystal teardrops, which always threatened to clink against one another but never actually did.

After the living room came a tremendously long corridor. There were a great many doors on each side of the corridor, and as Clara walked, she stretched her arms out to the side and let her hands idly drift across the doorknobs.

No, not that one, not that one . . . , she thought to herself as she ticked off each room in her head. When the corridor took a sharp turn, she came to a room on her right and stopped.

"Maybe." She turned the knob and entered.

Twisting all across the room, looping over and under itself, was a miniature roller coaster, its highest peak exactly over the room's door. On the far side, three roller-coaster cars, red, blue, and yellow, were waiting to be boarded. The walls were painted to look like a state fair, complete with sloppy, fat children eating corn dogs and a sinister-looking fortune-teller hunkered under a tent.

In the center of the room was a real cotton-candy machine, stacked high with paper cones. Clara turned it on, then expertly put the cone in the machine and let the candy billow up around it. She liked the sweet, hot smell and the sight of the whipping pink sugar. But once she had made the cone, she didn't really want to eat it. Still, it seemed the right sort of thing to have on a roller coaster, and she held on to it as she climbed into the first car—the red one—and pushed a button on its front panel. A great whirring motor started up, and loud music with a heavy beat began to play. The car lurched forward, trailing the other two behind it, and began a slow ascent up the first hill.

Clara's father had told her that she used to scream so loudly when she went on the roller coaster, he could hear her in his apartment below. She supposed it must be true, since her father never lied. Yet she could not remember ever having screamed on the roller coaster or anyplace else. In fact, there were so many things that Clara could not remember about being a child that she often wondered if something was terribly wrong with her. Did she have friends when she was little? Had her mother ever zipped up her jacket for her? Had her father ever picked her up when she cried? *Had* she ever cried? She had no idea. The past was so fuzzy. She might have asked her parents these things, but she was afraid they would consider her questions silly and childish, and she would not risk it.

Her first clear memory was of when she was eight years old. She tried on a pair of large dark sunglasses in a boutique on Fifth Avenue. Behind those glasses she could stare long

15

and hard at people in the store, and they never even noticed. She purchased the glasses, and soon after that she began to sit at her little round table in the back of Pish Posh, scanning the room for Nobodies.

Now, as the roller-coaster car climbed the first hill, Clara decided to try to scream. She held her cotton candy firmly in one hand, and at the moment the car began to fly down the hill, she opened her mouth and tested a small scream. It sounded like a toy poodle whose paw had been stepped on. She tried it again on the second hill. She opened her mouth wider, took a deep breath, and pushed. This time a real scream did come out, but it sounded horrible—like someone who had just discovered a dead body in their closet. And that brought her mind right back to Dr. Piff and his mystery, so she pushed the button in the front of the car. The car slowed down and came to a halt at the bottom of the ride.

The State Fair Room was no good, she decided, and she continued down the hallway to find another diversion. Over the years, her parents had consulted child experts to discover what children enjoyed. Then they had built the rooms accordingly. They reasoned that when Clara grew up and was attending a cocktail party where people were reminiscing about their childhoods, she could speak with authority on the thrill of the roller coaster and the taste of cotton candy. That way no one would think that she had had an odd, abnormal childhood, but she wouldn't have to go to actual amusement parks where there were all sorts of undesirable people wandering about.

A few doors down Clara paused to peer into the Day at the

Beach Room. The second she opened the door, a warm burst of salty ocean air assailed her nose. She slipped her shoes off and stepped inside, her bare feet sinking into the thick, pale sand. Beneath a giant beach umbrella was a giant beach towel splashed with giant pink and yellow flowers. Beside it was a cooler, which the cook replenished every day with Spam sandwiches (even though Clara never ate them). At the edge of the sand was "the ocean." It was a stretch of salt water, large enough to swim laps across and scarily deep at some points. A sound track played the caw-cawing of gulls and the occasional mother calling out to her child, "Don't go in too deep, Martha!" "Robbie, come let Mommy put some lotion on your back!" A special machine created waves, which were realistically large when the tide came in. In fact, the waves were crashing down very hard on the beach at the moment—too hard to swim in. Clara dipped her feet into the frothy edge. The water felt delightful against her toes, and she wondered what the real ocean looked like. She had never seen it. In fact, she had no memories of ever having been anywhere outside of Manhattan. Her father had promised to take her back to France one day, to visit her *grand-mère*, but the Frankofiles were always far too busy with the restaurant to travel.

A large wave splashed down hard in front of her and splattered her dress. Clara disapproved. Backing up, she frowningly examined the wet spot on her dress, and then left the Day at the Beach Room altogether.

She passed by the other rooms—the Haunted House Room, the Bumper Cars Room, the Giant Dollhouse Room, the Pie-Eating-Contest Room. Finally she came to a door at the very end of the corridor. The moment she saw it, she knew that it was exactly the room she was looking for. She opened the door. Inside was a single, solitary tree. It had been dug up from an ancient stretch of woods in Yungaburra, Australia, and transported to the Frankofiles' apartment. It had a massive trunk, and it was so tall that a special ceiling had been constructed, at the top of which was a gray-tinted plastic dome. This was the Tree Climbing Room.

Clara smiled. She loved that tree—perhaps because it lived alone in this room, strong and majestic and needing no one.

On the wall was a small hook that held a pair of overalls and a straw hat. According to the child experts, this was the fashion that simple country children wore when they climbed trees. Clara took off her dress and shoes and put on the overalls, then the hat, which she tied under her chin with its green ribbon.

There was a thick, nubby stump near the base of the tree on which to place your foot and boost yourself up to grasp the lowest branch. All along the length of the tree were thick branches spaced perfectly for a climbing child. Barefoot, Clara shimmied up the giant tree easily. She was not a child who was afraid of heights, and in fact, if she had been brought up in the country, she would have made a magnificent tree climber.

When she came close to the ceiling, Clara reached out and pressed a yellow button on the control panel set into the wall. Above her head, the plastic dome made a *clotch* sound. The dome began to separate in the center, the two sides pulling back and disappearing into the wall, laying bare the dark city sky.

Immediately, Clara could feel the breeze against her skin and smell the delightful semi-stinky city air (not stinky in a nasty way, but in the way the scalp of someone you're fond of smells). She climbed faster until she reached the very top, and then she nestled into a branch with a smooth crook in it. The tree was taller than the apartment building's roof, and her head was surrounded by the brilliant night stars.

Way down below, New York City shimmered with lights—store signs, streetlamps, traffic lights. It was as though the entire city stubbornly rebelled against the night, refusing to be blotted out by the darkness. Clara watched the starry, ceaseless movement of headlights from the cars and buses and taxis gliding through the streets. In the distance she could see an oblong, coal-black strip, which was Central Park. From this height, all the loud street noise was reduced to a smothered drone, except for the piercing wail of police sirens in the distance.

The warm breeze pushed at the brim of her straw hat and brushed delightfully against her bare feet. She wondered if country children felt like this all the time, and for a moment she experienced a pang of envy. But then she reminded herself that country children would not have a tree from Yungaburra, Australia, nor a bird's-eye view of New York City.

The sirens, which were faint at first, had grown louder. Now she could see the police cars weaving in and out of traf-

19

fic, until they finally stopped right in front of her building. She strained her eyes to see what was happening on the street below. The police officers had gotten out of their cars, and a woman ran up to them and started gesturing wildly. Suddenly all the policemen looked up.

Are they looking at *me?* Clara wondered. Because, indeed, they were looking right up toward the top of Clara's building. Other people on the street stopped and were pointing up in her direction.

They probably think I'm going to jump, Clara thought. How idiotic of them!

Then, out of the corner of her eye, Clara saw something moving along the roof of her building, below her. At first all she could make out was a patch of darkness. Was it a trick of light? But as she watched it, she began to make out a human form—slim and agile. It was moving around the edge of the roof, looking, it seemed, for a way down.

CHAPTER THREE

On the street below, an officer with a bullhorn shouted, "Listen up! There are fourteen police officers down here, and there's one of YOU! Those are not good odds!"

The figure on the roof stopped momentarily, then ran to the little service entrance that stood in one corner of the roof and pulled at the door. It was locked, but the person yanked and shoved on it for some minutes anyway.

Clara watched with great interest and surprisingly little fear. If you want to know the truth, Clara had a secret craving for danger, which was very unbecoming for such an elegant girl. But there are some things that one can't help. Her favorite movies always involved car chases along steep, winding cliffs and fistfights on the wings of airplanes.

Suddenly, the figure turned and looked at Clara's tree. The person walked toward it slowly; it would have been easy, at the distance of a few feet, to think that it was simply a tree planted on top of the roof, rather than one growing *through* the roof. In fact, the figure nearly toppled into the opening around the tree, which would have produced a very nasty fall into the Tree Climbing Room.

From Clara's vantage point, several feet above the roof, she saw the figure reach up and try to grab at a branch. The problem was that the hole in the roof was rather wide, and the branches were just out of the person's reach. The person jumped several times in the air but still could not reach any of the branches.

The voice in the bullhorn boomed: "Give yourself up! You are completely surrounded!" And that sounded so exactly like something out of a movie (in fact, it was: the officer with the bullhorn also liked action movies and had been waiting fifteen years for the chance to say those very words) that Clara actually laughed. It was just a small laugh—a snort, actually. But it was loud enough for the figure on the roof to hear.

"Is someone up there?" the person asked. It took Clara a minute to answer, not because she was afraid, but because she was shocked: the person's voice was that of a girl.

"Yes," Clara replied.

The girl hesitated for a minute, then stepped back and looked up. "Okay, I see you now." Her voice had a scratchy sound to it, which Clara found interesting. "What do you say you push that branch down a bit, just a few inches?"

Clara looked at the branch she was pointing to. She waited a minute, considering. More police sirens could be heard now, and when Clara glanced down at the street, it looked as if the entire precinct had come out for the event.

"Please, hey?" the girl said, and now her voice was tinged with panic. Clara climbed down a bit, and with her bare foot she pressed the branch down. The girl grabbed it and, with surprising nimbleness, swung herself up into the tree. Close now, Clara could get a better look at her. She looked about Clara's age, maybe a little older. She was tall and gangly with a flat face, which was damp with perspiration, and brown hair that reached just below her ears. She was hauling a fat backpack.

Clara could hear footsteps, lots of them, trampling up the stairs of the service entrance. Hurriedly, she scrambled a ways down the tree, past the girl, until she could reach the control panel on the wall. She punched the button and heard the *clotch* sound. The tinted-plastic dome stretched back over the top of the tree above them, smoothing itself out like one of those plastic rain bonnets that old ladies wear.

"Cripes! That's a first!" the girl said as she watched the dome snap shut over them, and Clara felt strangely pleased that she had impressed the girl.

The next moment they heard footsteps running on the roof and many voices all at once.

"Can they see us through the dome?" the girl whispered.

"I don't think so," Clara whispered back. But just in case, the girls stayed perfectly still. Clara felt her heart pounding so hard in her chest that it actually hurt. Soon the footsteps retreated and it grew silent.

"I think they're gone," the girl said, and she climbed down to a branch beside Clara's. "My name is Annabelle." She stuck out her hand.

"What were you doing on the roof?" Clara said without extending her own hand.

"When someone tells you their name, it's generally the custom to tell them *your* name back."

"You look familiar," Clara said in an accusatory way.

"Yeah? Well, I have that kind of face."

"No," Clara persisted. "I'm good with faces. I don't mix them up. I've met you before. What school do you go to?"

"What school *haven't* I gone to?" And as Annabelle began naming all the schools she had attended, it turned out that she had been to the Huxley Academy just a few months before, which was the very school that Clara attended.

"Why have you gone to so many schools?" Clara asked.

"I have a tendency to get suspended," she said, shrugging. "It drives my father insane. He's a genius himself, and he can't accept the fact that school and Annabelle just don't get along."

"A genius?" Clara said, always interested to discover a Somebody she had never heard of. "What sort of genius? What does he *do?*"

"Dad?" Annabelle tucked a hank of floppy hair behind her ear and smiled. "Oh, he's a thief."

Clara looked at Annabelle for a minute, wishing suddenly that she had her sunglasses on—it was always easier for her to tell if someone was lying when she was wearing her glasses. She inspected Annabelle's dark eyes but determined only that they looked steady and honest and even, much to Clara's surprise, quite intelligent.

"What does he steal?" Clara asked.

"This and that. It's changed over the years. He started by stealing cars, years and years ago, before I was born. Then he met my mom and she didn't like the hours he was working—when you steal cars you mostly have to work nights—so he started robbing banks. That way he could be home for dinner. But the problem with bank robbing is that you generally have to work with other bank robbers, and they're not the most reliable people in the world. They'll show up late for a robbery, or they'll forget to bring the masks, and sometimes they're really mean to the bank tellers. And besides, right after he became a bank robber, my mom divorced him, which meant the hours didn't matter anymore. Then my father became a jewel thief . . . so he'd be around a better class of people, you know? I started working with him a couple of years ago."

"You're a thief, too?"

"Hello! You're a bright one."

Clara didn't know which to be more shocked at—the fact that Annabelle was a criminal or that she had the nerve to speak to her in that way. But then she considered that it had been pretty thickheaded of her not to realize it. After all, Annabelle had fourteen police officers trying to arrest her while she was prowling around a rooftop in the middle of the night.

"What were you doing on the roof?" Clara asked again, swallowing back her pride.

"My dad and I were at a party on the thirtieth floor, and I had just robbed an apartment on the thirty-third floor. Dad broke into an apartment on the twenty-ninth floor. That's generally how we work. We get ourselves invited to parties in high-security buildings and then slip off and break into as many apartments as we can. But somebody must have had some kind of snazzy alarm system, because all of a sudden the police showed up and I had to scramble."

"But how do you get into the apartments?"

"Different ways. With this apartment building it's really easy. The terraces are close enough together that I can climb up from one to the next. You wouldn't believe how often people leave their terrace doors unlocked. Then I just swipe all the really good stuff"—she patted her fat backpack—"and climb back down to the apartment where the party is going on. Bing bang. Nothing fancy. You just can't be afraid of heights."

Clara squinted hard at Annabelle. "Why are you telling me all this? I could go to the police, you know."

"You?" Annabelle studied Clara for a moment. It reminded Clara of the way she watched the customers in the restaurant, which made her squirm a little.

Finally, Annabelle shook her head. "Nah, you're not the type. Well, I better get back to the party. Dad's probably done by now, too." Annabelle stuck out her hand again, which Clara now took. "Thanks, buddy. I owe you one. Nice hat, by the way."

Then she hitched up her backpack and climbed down the tree.

CHAPTER FOUR

Clara sat in the tree awhile longer, pondering what Annabelle had told her. Much as she tried to feel insulted, she was secretly pleased that Annabelle thought she was not "the type" to go to the police. Clara had always felt that, deep down, beneath her stylish black dresses and her good posture, she was bold—as bold as a girl like Annabelle. She smiled and snapped the straps of her overalls with her thumbs, in the same cocky way that she had seen fearless, wild country children do in the movies.

Thoroughly and delightfully exhausted, she climbed down and went to her bedroom. But just as she put on her nightgown, she noticed that the lid of her jewelry box was open. She walked over to it and looked inside. It was completely empty. A moist queasiness churned in her stomach. The Tahitian pearl necklace, the one she had been saving to add to her everyday outfit once she turned sixteen, was gone. She had searched high and low for the right pearls and finally found them a few months ago: pink-hued, nearly perfectly round pearls. Now they were gone.

Annabelle! She must have swiped them! In fact, she bet that it was her own "snazzy" alarm system that had tipped off the police.

She picked up the phone to dial 911. If she told them Annabelle's first name and the fact that she had once attended the Huxley Academy, they would certainly be able to track her down. But then she remembered that she had actually helped Annabelle escape into the tree, and that the only reason she knew Annabelle's name was that they had had a pleasant, casual conversation while the police were frantically searching the roof for her—a fact that would make Clara look very foolish indeed.

Her face reddened. Annabelle had been right. Clara wasn't the type to call the police. Not because she was too bold, but because she was too prideful. Annabelle had seen right through Clara, just as Clara saw through the customers at Pish Posh, and the realization was unpleasant to say the least.

She climbed into bed and pulled the covers over herself. For a long time she lay there, eyes open, while she nibbled at the ends of her hair, a thing she always did whenever she was deep in thought.

She thought about how that lousy, thieving Annabelle had sat in the tree with her, chatting to her like an old friend. And the worst of it, Clara had to admit, was that she had actually *liked* Annabelle. She couldn't even remember the last time she had liked someone.

She must have been laughing at me the whole time, Clara thought bitterly. She's probably lying in her own bed right now, thinking about what a sucker I am as she toys with my pearls. I can't stand the thought of it!

Clara hopped out of bed, opened up her closet, and pulled out a box that was on the top shelf. It contained stacks of old book reports and homework, school play programs, and yearbooks from the past two years. Sitting on the floor, she slowly and methodically went through everything, searching for Annabelle's last name. But there was nothing. It appeared that the girl had never gone to school long enough to have her name put on anything.

Never mind. I'll find her, Clara decided.

After that she fell asleep quite soundly, because she knew that when she was determined to do a certain thing, that thing was as good as done.

The following morning, after putting on Simple Black Dress #96 and adjusting her sunglasses so that they perched exactly a quarter inch down on the bridge of her nose, Clara buzzed the cook on the kitchen's intercom and informed her that she would be skipping breakfast. But as she passed the dining room and saw the customary pile of newspapers neatly stacked on the table, she changed her mind. She would not shirk her daily duty, not for some petty thief. She rang for the cook again and told her she would have breakfast after all, and in a few minutes' time the cook appeared at Clara's dining room table with a single poached egg, sourdough toast cut into triangles, and a glass of tomato juice.

Clara picked up the newspaper on top of the pile. It was the latest copy of *Hither & Thither*, a daily paper that tracked the comings and goings of all the important people in New York.

Recently they had added an amusing column called "Ask Ms. Mandy," where people wrote in with a famous person's name and Ms. Mandy would find out who their ancestors were. Today, someone had asked about a famous countess who lived on Park Avenue and bred Pekingese dogs.

"Well, folks, we have one naughty, naughty countess on our hands!" Miss Mandy replied to the letter. "Having researched her ancestors, it turns out our countess is not a real countess at all! Her family comes from New Jersey and her parents work in a hair dye factory. Perhaps she should 'fess up about her 'roots'!"

Clara snorted with disdain and not a little satisfaction. A good start to the day, since the fake countess was a customer at Pish Posh.

Not for long, Clara mused happily as she bit into her toast.

She went through all the papers very carefully, as she did every morning, watching for any other mention of Pish Posh customers. It was tedious work, true, but how else could she keep on top of things? And in the end, she was glad she had not skipped her morning ritual, because she found yet another article about a Pish Posh customer in the *Daily New Yorker*. It seemed that the well-known news anchorman John Sickle had been covering an earthquake in Japan. The accompanying film clip showed an injured woman lying on the ground with a rescue worker bending over her. Unfortunately, the rescue worker's pants drooped and a portion of his behind was visible, so when John Sickle had to say, "Witnesses reported several huge cracks," he burst out into uncontrollable giggles. The network quickly broke away to the sports segment, but angry phone calls immediately came pouring in from viewers. Sometimes there was an extremely fine line between a Nobody and a Somebody, and John Sickle had crossed it in the space of a few seconds. That could happen, if people weren't careful.

After she had finished going through the papers, Clara headed outside. The day was cool and fine, with fragments of bright blue sky peeking out between the buildings.

The Huxley Academy was about half a mile downtown. Clara considered taking a taxi, but she was still in high temper over Annabelle, and she thought that a walk might be just the thing to calm her down.

She walked past Pish Posh, which was closed now, and cut across Washington Square Park. The park was not really a square. It was more like a rectangle that was skirted by a wrought-iron fence. At its entrance was the great marble arch, which Clara's father liked to look at wistfully through the small kitchen window, sighing about how one day he would return to his beloved Paris, where the kitchen workers were not all so revolting.

Today, as Clara passed through the arch, she suddenly, out of the blue, remembered something Dr. Piff had told her when she was younger. More than two hundred years ago, he'd said, Washington Square Park was a burial ground for slaves and poor people, many of whom had died of yellow fever.

"Whenever I enter the park," he'd said, "I always tap my foot twice on the ground. Just so those old New Yorkers know that I'm thinking of them."

How odd that she'd remember something so trivial. And what a silly thing to do, on Dr. Piff's part! She frowned. It was unfortunate that Dr. Piff had popped into her thoughts when she had managed to block him and his mystery out of her mind all morning.

The park was crowded as usual. Some people were playing chess, others were watching a man juggling sneakers in front of the fountain, and dozens of people sprawled out on the grass, eating soft pretzels with salt the size of hailstones.

"Come have your portrait sketched!" called out a very short, slight man to anyone passing by. He was standing under a huge elm tree, surrounded by charcoal sketches of celebrities. The tree was very tall and ancient looking, and Clara had always been mesmerized by it. True, it wasn't nearly as tall as her climbing tree, but it had a strange, wizened look that made Clara wonder what it had seen in its long life. She found herself staring at it now, and the artist, encouraged by the fact that she had stopped near him, waved his arm wildly for her to come closer.

"Yes, come here, little one! I will draw your portrait. I will make you look like a movie star. Like her!" He held up a drawing of June Loblolly, a movie actress whom Clara had recently banished from Pish Posh. It was rather a good drawing of Ms. Loblolly, too. Her hair was whipping around her face in pale tendrils, and she looked terribly sad, as she always did in the movies.

"Ah, the extraordinary June Loblolly!" the artist exclaimed when he saw how intently Clara was studying the sketch. "She does not belong to our world, no?"

"I don't see what you mean," Clara said curtly, embarrassed that she had been caught staring.

"Why, she has a face that belongs to the ancient world, does she not?" he said, apparently amazed that she did not see this for herself. "You may see her likeness on the marble busts of Greek goddesses, gilded on Egyptian sarcophagi, carved into fertility fetishes unearthed in Peru. Not beautiful, perhaps, but full of wisdom, full of sadness, full of mercy!"

Clara was silent for a moment, and then drew herself up. "She's an actress. She can make herself look however she wants."

And with that, she turned and walked away, while the artist called after her, "Ten dollars for the drawing of June Loblolly, and a bargain at that! No? Okay, nine dollars!"

Perched on the edge of the fountain was a group of kids about her own age, talking with great animation. What in the world did they have to say to each other? Clara pondered. Nothing important, certainly. Yet she suddenly wondered if Annabelle sometimes sat with groups of kids like this one. Maybe she'd tell them about the stupid girl who saved her from the police, right after she had stolen the same girl's own pearls. This fired up Clara's temper once again and she began to walk faster, nearly crashing into a woman on Rollerblades.

After she crossed the park, she made her way up two avenue blocks to the Huxley Academy. The academy's building had been an orphanage for little girls years and years ago, and it looked a little like a miniature castle, with its heavy gray stone walls and its massive oak doors, over which crouched sinister gargoyles. It was the sort of place where one might expect to see tapestries hanging on the walls and footmen holding candles and maybe a princess or two passing through the dimly lighted hallways. But instead, the school was remarkably ordinary inside, with excellent lighting and no footmen.

The halls were very quiet, but Clara could hear the faint murmur of voices somewhere. It was an eerie sound that made her think about the orphans who used to live here more than a hundred years ago. She imagined for a moment that she was hearing their ghostly voices now, drifting sadly through the hallways, and the image was so vivid that she nearly succeeded in frightening herself right back out of the building. But then she came to her senses and reminded herself that the voices were coming from the end of the hall, and that they belonged to the kids who had failed courses during the year and were now being forced to repeat them over the summer.

She headed down the hall to the main office, a small cubicle where the principal conducted his business. She tried the door, but it was locked and, peering through the little window in the door, she could see that the room was dark and empty.

"Can I help you?" asked a tall, long-limbed woman with a mass of unkempt light brown, curly hair. She had stepped out of the teacher's lounge, across the hall from the principal's office. She was wearing a gaudy red-and-green-striped pantsuit and was carrying a mug of coffee. "Oh! Clara Frankofile! Well, it's been an age!"

"Hi, Ms. Blurt," Clara said unenthusiastically to her former art teacher.

"I was just thinking about you . . . just the other day. I was reading something . . . hmm, now what was it?"

"I need to talk to the principal, Miss Blurt," Clara cut her short.

"Ooh, the principal," Miss Blurt said. "Mmm. Nooooo. Nope! He is on vacation, our principal. He went to . . . now where was it? . . . Someplace where there is water . . . and fish! Yes, many, many fish . . . but I can't for the life of me . . . Now, what was I reading the other day when I thought of you, Clara?"

Clara sighed. This was not working out as she had planned. Once again she had a vision of Annabelle laughing at her, and she felt her cheeks grow warm.

"I need to find out where one of my old schoolmates lives, Ms. Blurt," Clara said, trying to muffle the anger in her voice. "She was a friend of mine. We lost touch when she left the school."

"Fizzelli!" Ms. Blurt thrust her coffee mug in the air victoriously, and some of the coffee sloshed out onto the floor.

"No, her name is Annabelle."

"I mean the article I was reading. Caleb Fizzelli. Yes, that's it! I was reading about Caleb Fizzelli, one of my favorite painters of the nineteenth century. Sadly, he isn't very well known. In fact, I doubt most people have even heard of him, but there was an eensie little article in one of my art magazines that mentioned him. And guess what that article said?"

Clara sighed. "Really, I have no idea."

"The article said that he lived in the very same spot where the Pish Posh restaurant now stands, way back in the 1800s. 'Pish Posh!' I said to myself. 'Well, that's the restaurant that Clara Frankofile's parents own.' Isn't that marvelous!"

"Ms. Blurt," Clara tried again. "Do you remember a girl named Annabelle? Tall, thin. Raspy voice."

"Mmm. Ann-a-belle. Yes, I do remember a girl . . . very untalented artist. She did something odd with people's nostrils. Drew them very large and piglike. Don't know why—"

"Do you remember her last name?"

"Oh, my. You know, I can remember the names of artists who have been dead for hundreds of years, but I do have such a difficult time with the names of people who are still alive. The curse of an art teacher, I suppose!"

"She must be listed somewhere in the school records. Can't we look it up?" She nodded toward the locked office. Ms. Blurt suddenly grew serious, clutching her coffee mug to her chest with both hands.

"I'm afraid school records are private, Clara," she said solemnly. "Regulations, after all." Clara examined Ms. Blurt carefully. She had a gift for seeing through people, and now she tried to figure out just *how* strictly Ms. Blurt would follow regulations.

"Of course, I understand." Clara nodded, equally solemn. "Thanks anyway." She started to walk away, then stopped and turned back to Ms. Blurt. "You know, now that I think about it, a busboy at Pish Posh once found a funny little sketch on the wall in the kitchen's linen room. Do you think that artist, Fizz, Fizz—"

"Fizzelli." Ms. Blurt blinked three times in rapid succession, her face suddenly animated.

"—Fizzelli. Do you think he might have drawn it?"

"Oh, indeed he may have! Oh, indeed! Wouldn't that be remarkable! If I could only see it, I could tell for sure." Ms. Blurt's coffee spilled all over her hand, but she was so excited, she didn't seem to notice.

"I could arrange for you to come to the restaurant. You could have some dinner, and then look at the drawing. We do have a strict policy about reservations, but I suppose I could break the regulations for you, Ms. Blurt. If you could break them for me . . ."

Ms. Blurt bit at her bottom lip. Clearly, the temptation was very great. She stared down at her coffee, much of which was now on the floor and splattered across her striped pants, as though she'd find the answer to her dilemma in her mug. "To take a peek at the sketch—that would be most educational."

"I'm sure the principal would agree," Clara said.

"He might be upset if I *didn't* do it," Ms. Blurt muttered to herself. After a moment, she said, "Hold this," and handed her coffee cup to Clara. She pulled out a ring of keys from her pocket, opened the principal's office, and then shut herself in the room.

Clara could hear the clatter of metal file drawers opening

and closing, then the rustle of paperwork. After a while, Ms. Blurt emerged with a scrap of paper and handed it to Clara. On it was written "Annabelle Arbutnot, 55 West 86th Street."

Clara smiled. Well, Annabelle was in for a surprise.

She handed the mug back to Ms. Blurt without a word and started to hurry back down the hall.

"When should I come to the restaurant?" Ms. Blurt called after her.

"Tonight is fine," Clara called back without stopping.

"But what should I wear?" Ms. Blurt asked.

"Whatever you like," Clara called back hastily, then wondered if that was the best advice. But she was in too much of a hurry to worry about it.

CHAPTER FIVE

Clara hailed a taxi. The driver eyed her suspiciously as she climbed into the backseat.

"You got money on you, kid?"

"No, I'm going to pay you with crayons. Of course I have money, you boob! Now take me to Fifty-five West Eighty-sixth Street immediately."

"Nice mouth!" the driver sniped. But he took her straight up to Eighty-sixth Street in double time, snaking in and out of traffic, and coming so close to ramming into other cars that several times Clara had to shut her eyes and clutch the door handle. The taxi finally came to a halt in front of a brownstone on a quiet, tree-lined street, off Columbus Avenue.

"Fifty-five West Eighty-sixth Street, kid." Clara paid the man and gave him a large tip, just because he probably thought she wouldn't.

It was a pretty little brownstone, with stone urns filled with flowers lining the front staircase's balustrade. She walked up the steps. To the left of the door was a bronze placard that read Dr. JOHN S. ARBUTNOT. Doctor? Annabelle had said he was a thief. Maybe Ms. Blurt had given her the address of the wrong Annabelle.

Clara propped her dark glasses on top of her head—something she always did when she was unsure of herself—and squinted against the brightness of the day, contemplating whether or not to press the doorbell.

"Cripes, how'd you find me?" said a scratchy voice from behind her. "Hold this a minute, will you?" Annabelle had come up the steps, hugging a bag of groceries. She pushed the bag at Clara, which Clara, momentarily caught off guard by Annabelle's sudden appearance, took. Annabelle reached into her shirt and pulled out a chain with keys attached to them.

"You stole my pearl necklace," Clara said, suddenly remembering why she was there.

"Of course I did," Annabelle agreed without a trace of guilt as she put the key in the door.

"Well, I want it back," Clara demanded furiously just as Annabelle pushed open the door.

"Oh, sure. No problem," Annabelle replied casually, taking the bag of groceries out of Clara's hands. "Fair is fair. Come on in. Have some lunch." She clearly was not disturbed by Clara's surprise appearance, which made Clara even angrier.

"And how dare you—"

"Shh. Keep it down. My dad's got a client in his office." They walked through a short foyer, past a closed door through which muffled voices could be heard, and into the kitchen. Annabelle plopped the bag down on the kitchen counter and began putting its contents—packages of odd and unappetizing-looking food—into the fridge.

"I thought you said your father was a thief." Clara narrowed her eyes at Annabelle. "The sign outside said *Doctor*."

"Don't believe everything you read," Annabelle said, putting away a box marked ORGANIC RED-GREEN ALGAE FLAKES. "So . . . you hungry? You want a sandwich? We've got mung-bean salad, some diced wheat gluten . . . I think there's still some marinated tempeh left—"

"All I want from you is my necklace."

Annabelle sighed and tucked her hair behind her ears. "Sheesh, I just thought you might be hungry. Okay, just wait here. I'll go get it."

Left alone in the kitchen, Clara folded her arms and waited, flabbergasted by how nonchalant Annabelle was. In fact, Annabelle seemed almost glad to see her, like they were old friends. Ha! Like she would ever be friends with a thief! Not likely.

Suddenly, Clara heard the sound of a woman's voice, crying out boldly, "But I *do* hear voices in my head, sir! I hear them as clearly as I hear your own!" It was coming from Annabelle's father's office.

"You are lying," came the harsh response from a man—Annabelle's father, Clara guessed. "You just want me to *believe* you are insane. Instead, you are simply an evil, no-goodnik, snot-nosed pig of a woman! I can't bear the sight of you! Fleechhh!"

Clara covered her mouth to keep from gasping. This man was horrible. Horrible!! And the woman must be his patient, too. She had come to him for help, and he was treating her so cruelly!

Clara quietly inched closer to the office door and leaned her ear against the wall outside, to hear better. The woman was crying softly now, but her voice still had great strength in it as she declared, "Upon my honor, it doesn't matter what you think of me."

Good for you! Clara thought, nodding.

"You are wrong, mademoiselle!" Annabelle's father shouted. "It matters very much what I think of you. And now you will see just *how* much!" There was a moment of utter silence, and then the woman began to scream in the most bloodcurdling way, so that Clara actually jumped and pressed her hands against her mouth to keep from shrieking.

"Do you feel the flames licking at your toes, mademoiselle? Do you feel the fire creeping up your legs now? Go ahead and struggle against those ropes—it will only make the flames leap higher! You will burn for your lies! You will writhe in eternal torment!" And all the while the woman never stopped screaming, until Clara could stand it no longer and burst into the office.

CHAPTER SIX

Lying on an overstuffed lavender couch was a blonde young woman with an expensive-looking haircut. Her hands, with their tapered, bright pink nails, were folded in her lap, and her eyes, which were shut when Clara first entered, were now open wide and staring at Clara in surprise. Opposite her was a pleasant-looking man with thick, light brown hair and a neatly trimmed beard and mustache.

"Pardon me, but I'm afraid you'll have to leave," the man said kindly. "We're in the middle of a session."

"I heard a woman screaming," Clara said.

"Was I screaming?" the woman on the couch asked eagerly.

"Only a little, Amber," the man said. "Which is perfectly understandable, since you were being set on fire."

"Cool!" Amber said as she pulled a pack of gum out of the pocket in her blouse. "And was I brave at the end?" She peeled a stick of gum and popped it in her mouth.

"Wonderfully brave, Amber. You hardly flinched." Then he turned to Clara. "Now, if you'll excuse us." Clara was so confused, it took her a moment to nod in embarrassment and leave.

Just as she closed the door softly behind her, Annabelle came trotting down the hallway, holding a paper bag.

"Ho, there! What were you doing in my father's office?"

"I . . . I heard screams."

"Oh." Annabelle rolled her eyes. "That's Amber, one of Dad's clients. Such a drama queen! She was Joan of Arc in another life, and she insists on repeating the whole burning-at-the-stake thing again and again. You'd think once would be enough, wouldn't you? She says it's helping her to quit smoking."

"What are you talking about?" Clara said. "Why was your father being so mean to her?"

"That's his job. He's a hypnotherapist." She looked at Clara as if that would explain everything, but when she saw that it clearly didn't, she continued to explain. "He hypno-tizes people to help them get rid of their problems. You know, like if someone wants to lose weight or stop smoking or get over their fear of elevators. But he also can get peo-ple to remember who they were in their past lives. Oh, they can remember all kinds of weird stuff—like being a soldier in the Civil War or owning a pastry shop in France during the Revolution."

"But how do you know they're not faking it?"

"Some of them fake it, but my dad has ways to tell if they are. Lately, everybody wants to have lived during medieval times. And then there are all the people who say they were famous in their past lives, like Queen Elizabeth or Cleopatra or something. I mean, what are the chances of that? The ones who are *really* hypnotized usually find out that they had average, boring lives in the past, just like their lives now."

"So Amber is faking it?" Clara nodded toward the door.

"Oh, no. She really was Joan of Arc. She's one of two 'dead celebrity' patients he has. The other one is William Shakespeare, but he's a lot more fun than Joan of Arc. At least he knows a few good jokes."

"But," Clara said after a moment, "I thought you said your father was a thief."

"Shh!" Annabelle grabbed her roughly by the elbow. She was a good head taller than Clara, and quite strong, and although Clara resisted, she found herself unceremoniously dragged down the hallway and out the front door.

"Well . . . is he or isn't he?" Clara insisted, once Annabelle had released her on the landing of the front steps. Annabelle crossed her arms against her chest, leaned back against the balustrade, and narrowed her eyes at Clara.

"How did you find us anyway?"

"I persuaded someone at the Huxley Academy to give me your address," Clara said evasively.

"*Persuaded?*"

"I bribed her," Clara admitted.

"I knew you were a shrewd duck!" Annabelle said approvingly. Clara would have objected, but it secretly pleased her. "Hey, what's your name, by the way?"

"Clara."

"Clara? Funny name for a kid. Yeah, Dad is a thief, sure," Annabelle said. "But how do you think we get invited to rich people's parties? I mean, who's going to invite a thief into their house? So Dad learned how to be a hypnotherapist by reading books. Plus, he's a genius and can do anything he sets his mind to."

"Then why doesn't he just become a hypnotherapist and give up being a thief?" Clara asked. It seemed an obvious enough question, but Annabelle looked at Clara like she'd just suggested that her dad lick an electrical outlet.

"Where's the sense in that?!" she exclaimed angrily, kicking one of the stone flowerpots. "I mean, that would ruin everything. What would I do? Go back to *school?* Join the debating team and trade friendship bracelets? No thank you."

In a way, Clara could understand Annabelle perfectly. She would have felt the same if someone suggested that she spend less time at Pish Posh and do things other kids her age did. But the mention of bracelets made her remember why she was there in the first place, and her former indignation returned.

"I thought you said you were getting my jewelry," she said sternly.

"Oh, right. Here." Annabelle handed her the paper bag. Clara opened it promptly. Inside was the Tahitian pearl necklace. Clara should have felt victorious; but she didn't. For some reason, the pearls seemed less important now that she had them back.

"Fine. That's all I wanted. Good-bye," Clara said. She felt a sudden cramp in her stomach. She must be getting sick. Summer flu. She got one every year. Tomorrow she would be sneezing and achy and would have to stay in bed all day.

The front door opened and Amber stepped out, with Annabelle's father behind her. "I'll see you next week, Amber," he said. "Just stay away from fire for twenty-four hours—no barbecues, no campfires."

Amber blew a thin bubble with her gum, then snapped it. "You're the best, Doc."

"And no cigarettes," he called after her when she reached into her bag and pulled out a pack. But she pretended not to hear him as she strode off down the street.

"Poor Joan of Arc is probably rolling over in her grave," Annabelle's father said, shaking his head. Then he winked at Clara and pinched Annabelle's nose and went back inside.

"So, Clara," Annabelle said, "will you come back to visit me again?"

"Possibly," Clara said. She adjusted her sunglasses. As she walked down the stairs, she began to feel better. Much better. Miraculously, the summer flu had instantly left her body.

CHAPTER SEVEN

Every table at the Pish Posh restaurant was occupied that evening, as usual. Clara sat at her little round table in the back, trying hard to focus on ferreting out the Nobodies, but she kept thinking about Dr. Piff. Pish Posh was different without him. You wouldn't think his absence would matter so much since Dr. Piff was such a quiet and plain man. But somehow Pish Posh seemed a little less glittery and fabulous when he wasn't there.

You have failed to notice a most peculiar and mysterious thing that is happening right under your nose.

Clara thought about Dr. Piff's words again and gazed around the restaurant. What could be so peculiar and mysterious?

Her eye caught Mavis Von Mavis, the famous artist, who was eating at a table in the corner with someone whose portrait she had been painting. Mavis Von Mavis held up a brussels sprout and cried, "This is the exact shade of green I will use for your face!" Then she dropped the brussels sprout into her bra for safekeeping, while the woman whose face was going to be painted brussels-sprout green looked decidedly unhappy.

Mavis Von Mavis was certainly peculiar. But so were many of the other customers at Pish Posh.

Just then the restaurant's door opened and in walked Ms. Blurt, dressed in a purple velvet pantsuit. Cinching her waist was a shiny red belt with the words SASSY LADY . . . SASSY LADY . . . SASSY LADY . . . printed all around it. She had attempted to tame her light brown curls by pinning them up here and there, but the effect was that she looked as though she had clumps of caramel corn stuck to her head.

Oh, no, Clara thought, I forgot all about Ms. Blurt!

Up front, Clara's mother was staring at Ms. Blurt with wide, incredulous eyes. Ms. Blurt said something to her, and Lila looked down at the reservation book, then shook her head vigorously.

Clara got up to explain the situation to her mother, and the moment she rose, all conversation stopped and every eye in the restaurant turned to her in dread. Everyone thought she had found a Nobody.

"You are not in our book, Ms. Blah," Lila Frankofile was saying.

"Blurt," Ms. Blurt corrected her. "Clara Frankofile invited me to dine here tonight." Her voice resounded loudly in the silence.

"Is this true, Clara?" Lila Frankofile looked appalled, and some of the customers murmured, "Clara Frankofile invited *that* to Pish Posh? Impossible!" and "She looks just like a stick of grape chewing gum in that outfit."

Ms. Blurt blushed to nearly the same shade of red as her Sassy Lady belt and looked at Clara helplessly. Clara hesitated. Ms. Blurt was so obviously a Nobody. In fact, you would be hard-pressed to find someone who was more a Nobody than Ms. Blurt. What would everyone think if Clara admitted that she'd personally invited Ms. Blurt to Pish Posh? Clara opened her mouth, then closed it, cleared her throat, and looked down at the floor.

"I guess I must have misunderstood," Ms. Blurt said finally. She gave her belt a sad little tug and turned to leave.

"Wait," Clara said to Ms. Blurt. Then to her mother, "It's true. I invited her to have dinner at the restaurant tonight."

"Clara, how could you?!" Lila was aghast. "And in any case, we are completely full. There's not a table to spare."

"She'll dine at my table," Clara said decisively.

"Impossible!" Lila cried. But Clara hated to be told that she could not do something, so rather imperiously she hooked her arm through Ms. Blurt's and ushered her to the little round table in the back of the restaurant. One of the waiters rushed to bring a second chair to the table, and Ms. Blurt, still red in the face, sat down. Every customer fell to whispering, filling the restaurant with a sound that was uncannily like that of an industrial washing machine—*phiddle slush, phiddle slush.*

Clara ordered onion soup and braised lamb and roast Cornish hen and sautéed truffles and spinach quiche and asparagus spears in hollandaise sauce and chocolate mousse cake and crème brûlée and raspberry tart with vanilla ice cream, and much more—so much, in fact, that the waiter had to set up a little cart beside their table to hold it all. And the whole time, all the famous and glamorous people in the restaurant stole surreptitious glimpses at this woman who was *so very* important that Clara Frankofile herself had invited her to dine at her table.

Ms. Blurt declared that she had never in her life tasted anything so delicious, and she tasted it ALL until her belly began to bulge beneath her purple pantsuit so that she looked a little like a bug. It was only when she had had a bite of every dessert on the menu (well, maybe two bites) that she asked about Caleb Fizzelli's drawing on the wall.

"Can I see it now, do you suppose?" Ms. Blurt asked.

Pierre Frankofile never allowed customers into his kitchen—no exceptions. It didn't matter if you were a movie star or a king. But Clara was feeling especially contrary tonight. She smiled, imagining the look on the other customers' faces if she brought Ms. Blurt back there.

"Why not," Clara declared, and she led Ms. Blurt in through the kitchen to the astounded looks of everyone, including her mother.

As usual, Pierre Frankofile was screaming at one of the cooks, so he didn't notice right away that a customer was in his kitchen.

"You ham-brained, slobbering pimple! I will stick your head in a pot of boiling pasta water if you ever do that again, you web-footed—"

"Papa," Clara interrupted loudly enough to make her father turn away from his victim, who was taking the abuse relatively calmly. "Papa, this is Ms. Blurt, and she is here to see that drawing on the wall."

Pierre took one look at Ms. Blurt and his already pink, angry face turned a shade of dark violet. He glared at her for a moment, speechless.

"*Sacre bleu!*" he screamed finally, his eyes bulging. "And how would she like it if while she was looking at that drawing, I took out my paring knife and cut off her—"

"And *I* want her to see it, Papa," Clara said firmly, for she was not afraid of her father at all, since he was generally all hot air and nonsense and had never really cut off anybody's appendages.

"Victor," Clara called to a short, burly man with a cracked front tooth. "You were the one who found that drawing on the wall, weren't you?"

"S'right."

"Please show us where it is."

Victor gazed questioningly at Pierre.

"Show them where it is, Victor," Pierre cried, "or so help me I will bite off the tip of your nose, chew it up, and spit it into the East River!"

"Yes, sir." They followed Victor through a door near the back of the kitchen and into a little side room. Lining every wall were stacks and stacks of crisp white linen tablecloths and napkins, wrapped in plastic and piled one on top of the other. The stacks were twice as tall as Clara, and not an inch of wall space could be seen between them.

"S'round here somewhere," Victor said. Stack by stack,

he took down the fortress of linen, revealing the wall a bit at a time. Finally, toward the bottom of one wall, faint markings appeared, and once Victor had removed all the stacks, the painting could be seen clearly.

It was a painting of a garden, with a crescent moon hanging over it, and two figures sitting on a bench. The details were shadowy, since the painting was only sketchily done, as though the artist had only just started to work on it before abandoning the project.

Ms. Blurt knelt down and examined it, making small sounds the whole time, until she declared the drawing "most definitely a Fizzelli. Oh, my!"

She stared at it for a good long time, until Victor began to shift his legs around impatiently. Taking the hint, Ms. Blurt stood up and brushed the linen lint off of her pantsuit.

"He must have intended to make a fresco—a painting on plaster—and never finished it," she said, her face flushed with excitement as they made their way out of the room and back into the kitchen.

"Thank you, Mr. Frankofile." Ms. Blurt nearly curtsied to him. "And I'm sorry to disturb you all . . . ," she said to the rest of the kitchen staff, but her voice trailed off when her eyes fell on Audrey, who was chopping escarole. Ms. Blurt stared at Audrey for a moment, her lips parted in surprise. Audrey looked up and squinted at her through her thick glasses, then abruptly turned her back to Ms. Blurt and dropped the escarole in a pot on the stove.

"What's wrong?" Clara asked.

"Who is that?" Ms. Blurt whispered to Clara.

"Nobody. Just the woman who makes the soup."

"Ask her to turn around," Ms. Blurt said with urgency.

"What for?"

"Just ask her." There was a rare tone of authority in Ms. Blurt's voice, one that she had never used even in the classroom.

"Audrey!" Clara called loudly to be heard above the clatter of plates and steamy roar of the dishwasher. "Audrey, turn around!" But to Clara's great surprise, the young woman utterly and willfully ignored her.

This act of disobedience caught Pierre's attention, and he flung a spatula at the soup cook, hitting her on the back, and boomed, "Turn around!!"

Slowly and reluctantly, Audrey turned around and faced Ms. Blurt. Ms. Blurt gazed at her, her eyes growing wider.

"Oh . . . but . . . how can it be? . . ." she muttered right before her legs buckled and she passed out on the kitchen floor.

CHAPTER EIGHT

The busboy wadded up a kitchen apron and put it under Ms. Blurt's head, and Clara dabbed at her face with a wet kitchen rag.

"Ms. Blurt . . . Ms. Blurt . . . ," Clara said.

"Slap her," suggested Pierre.

"Ms. Blurt, open your eyes," Clara pleaded.

"Poke the bottoms of her feet with the meat fork," Pierre said. He began to search in his utensil drawer for a meat fork, when Ms. Blurt's eyes fluttered, then opened fully.

"Are you all right, Ms. Blurt? You fainted," Clara said.

Ms. Blurt struggled to raise herself up. With Clara's help, she got to her feet and adjusted her belt.

"Much better now! Yes. Thank you," she sputtered, her eyes nervously darting at Audrey and then away again. "I'll be on my way." She headed out the kitchen door and Clara followed, perplexed, while Pierre called after her, "I still think a quick slap would do her good."

All the customers turned to gawp at the illustrious

Ms. Blurt, but she did not appear to notice their stares. She said a hasty good-bye to Clara, thanking her for the meal and the sight of the little drawing, and hurried out the front door.

Clara hesitated for a moment. Then she went after her, following Ms. Blurt, who was already halfway up the block, heading uptown, her reedy legs working double time. Clara had to break into an all-out run to catch up with her, and when she grabbed the velvet-clad elbow, Ms. Blurt shrieked.

"It's just me, Ms. Blurt."

"I really must be going." She pulled out of Clara's grasp with surprising strength and began to hurry off again.

"What did you see back in the kitchen that startled you?" Clara pursued as she rushed to keep pace with her.

"Nothing," Ms. Blurt said shortly, without slowing down.

"I don't like secrets, Ms. Blurt. Tell me what you saw!" Clara demanded.

Ms. Blurt stopped then, so quickly in fact that Clara suddenly found that she was walking by herself and had to turn around and walk back.

"That woman in the kitchen . . . ," Ms. Blurt said. "What do you know about her?"

Clara shrugged. "Hardly anything. She's worked at Pish Posh since it opened, and she lives in the apartment above the kitchen. But that's all. Ms. Blurt, what is this about?"

Ms. Blurt's large blue eyes looked at Clara carefully. She seemed about to say something, but then simply shook her head and smiled apologetically. "Pay no attention to me, Clara. My imagination sometimes gets the better of me."

• • •

Clara went to bed that evening feeling strangely at odds. Though she lay still for a good hour in the silent apartment, she was unable to sleep. Her thoughts kept tumbling restlessly over the mystery of Ms. Blurt's reaction to Audrey. Was this part of the strange and peculiar thing that Dr. Piff had talked about?

Finally, when she could no longer stand lying there in the dark and staring up at the ceiling, she jumped out of bed. A good, strenuous climb and the night air might tire her out, she reasoned, and she headed toward the Tree Climbing Room. But once she opened the door, she realized that she had been secretly hoping to meet up with Annabelle again.

How ridiculous! Clara thought, shaking her head. What are the chances that Annabelle will be on the roof again tonight? And why should I even care? The girl is a Nobody from head to toe.

Angry at herself, she stepped back out of the room and slammed the door. She walked back down the hallway restlessly, finally pausing in front of a room that she hadn't visited for a long time. It was the Neighborhood in Brooklyn Room. When she was younger, she used to visit this room quite often, but as she got older, she had simply lost interest. She hesitated a minute, then turned the doorknob and walked in.

The room was completely dark, which made her wonder if her parents had "retired" it. They did that sometimes when they thought a room was bad for Clara in some way, like the Blueberry Picking Room, which they retired because the blueberries stained Clara's fingers to the point where she could not be seen in public.

But then she remembered the way that the Neighborhood in Brooklyn Room worked. You had to walk in, close the door, and wait—which she did. After a moment she began to detect the odor of bacon frying and coffee brewing. Then the street-lamps began to light up very slowly—a morning in Brooklyn—and she could make out the shapes of low buildings with stoops and tiny, fenced-in gardens in front of them, and a street sign that said AVENUE U and EAST 7TH STREET. There was the bakery with the heaps of pastries and cookies and cakes displayed in the windows. And there was a pizza shop, with its tall red-and-white-striped tables and stools for customers. None of it was real—not the pastries, which were made of glazed ceramic, and not the gardens with their silk flowers, or the shellacked slices of fake pizza. But the smells were real, even if they were pumped through an exhaust system.

And now the sounds—the *burrr* of cars passing, people calling to each other in rough, loud, rude voices, dogs barking. It was all somehow delightfully soothing. She climbed the stairs to one of the houses and sat down in a lawn chair on the front porch, leaned her head back, and shut her eyes. Before long she felt herself drifting off to sleep.

"*Mais oui!* There you are!" Pierre Frankofile burst into the room, still dressed in his chef's uniform. His entrance awakened Clara, and she sat bolt upright in the lawn chair.

"Oh," she said, rubbing her eyes, "hi, Papa. What are you doing here?" It was very strange for her father to visit her in her apartment.

"I just wanted to see what happened with your friend . . . Ms. Bloat . . ."

"Blurt. She's fine."

"Is she?" He rubbed his hands together. "Did you slap her?"

"No."

Her father looked disappointed, and Clara realized that that was probably what he had come to find out. And, in fact, it did appear that he was about to leave, but he suddenly changed his mind, walked up the stairs to the porch, and sat beside Clara in a lawn chair. The light from the streetlamps was still dim, an early morning light, even though it was actually nearly midnight outside. But it was very convincing, and Clara really did feel like the day was just beginning, rather than ending.

"Nice room," her father said. "Makes one feel homesick somehow." He turned to her and smiled. "It reminds me of the little village in France where I was born—you know, the smells, the sound of *les enfants* playing. One day, when I have the time, I'd like to take you there to see it, to meet your *grand-mère* . . ." He shut his eyes and seemed to drift off in his own reverie.

"Papa," Clara said.

"Mmm?" he asked without opening his eyes.

"What do you know about Audrey?"

"Audrey Aster?" His face lost its dreaminess, and he frowned. "I know she makes a tolerable soup, when she isn't lazing around like a bespectacled sloth."

"What do you know about *her*, though? Where does she come from? Does she have a family? Things like that."

"How on earth should I know?" Pierre looked at his daughter with bewilderment, as though she had asked him what he knew about earthworms.

"Where did she work before you hired her?" Clara persisted.

"Where, what, how?!" Pierre's voice had reached its usual restaurant boom by now. "I have no idea! It was Dr. Piff who brought her to me."

"Dr. Piff?" Clara sat up.

"Years ago, when we first opened. He said that she needed work and that she would not disappoint me—oh, what a lie! They are a lousy, putrid lot, the whole bunch of them. If I had my way, I would tie them all to a tree and . . ."

Clara sank back down in the lawn chair. Once her father began on a rant, there was no stopping him. He bellowed on and on, drowning out the taped neighborhood noises, making the lawn chair squeak every time he threw up his hands to show how he would throttle the busboy or tear the pastry chef into a thousand pieces, until, finally exhausted, he wiped the sweat from his forehead with the bottom of his chef's jacket and stood up.

"Well, *bon soir*, Clara, I'm completely done in." He gave her a quick peck on the top of her head and left her alone. Well, not quite alone. Now she had some new ideas to keep her company.

Dr. Piff, huh? . . .

CHAPTER NINE

That morning Clara passed the dining room, eyed the stack of waiting newspapers on the table, and decided that they could wait.

"No breakfast today," she called hastily to the cook as she passed the kitchen and headed directly to Pish Posh.

Lila Frankofile was sitting at the restaurant's bar, deep in thought. Lila wasn't generally there that early, but she had a touchy situation to deal with: the princess of Macedonia was to be there that evening at the same time as her sister, the empress of Bulgaria. The two of them were known to detest each other, and whenever they were in the same place at the same time, a fistfight invariably erupted. Lila scratched at her head as she stared at the reservation book, trying to figure out the best way to keep the two sisters from getting within sparring distance of each other.

When Clara walked in, Lila looked up briefly and commented, "A bit early today, aren't you? Did you happen to see today's edition of *Hither & Thither*?"

The newspaper was on the bar, its cover featuring a large

photo of several women with no eyebrows. The headline read "Jousting Match Will Benefit Medieval Costume Exhibit at the Metropolitan Museum of Art." Clara started to read the article out loud: "All of society's most glamorous ladies have ripped out their eyebrows—"

"Not that," Lila interrupted. "Look at the article below."

The article below read,

> "Seen at Pish Posh! Who was the mystery woman who dined with the elusive and exclusive young Clara Frankofile? Miss Frankofile, who NEVER dines with anyone, even went so far as to give the mystery woman (who was dressed in an ultratrendy velvet pantsuit with a belt inscribed with 'Sassy Lady') a tour of the kitchen. Unheard of!! Is she foreign royalty? Is she an up-and-coming actress? All of New York City is dying to know!"

"How idiotic." Clara rolled her eyes.

"You must bring your friend back to dine," Lila said decisively.

"But she's just an art teacher."

"Don't be a snob, dear. Some Somebodies are born and some Somebodies are made. If *Hither & Thither* has made an art teacher into a Somebody, who will know the difference?"

"I will!" Clara was shocked that her mother could accept an imposter. She threw the newspaper down and went into the kitchen. It was empty, too early for the workers, or her father, to be there. Everything looked peaceful. The stoves were gleaming, having been scrubbed the night before by the workers. The massive dishwasher, which usually spewed out a thick wall of steam and sounded like a hundred electric pencil sharpeners all going at the same time, was now simply a quiet metal box. In just a few hours, it would be chaos here again.

Clara opened a metal door in the back of the kitchen and went up a flight of stairs, a side entrance to the apartment on the second floor. At the landing was a short hallway, and at the end of the hallway was a door. Clara pushed the buzzer and waited. There was no answer, but she thought she could hear someone moving around inside. She pushed it again, three times in a row, and then knocked loudly.

Finally, the door opened and Audrey the soup cook stood there in a pair of jeans, a sleeveless white tank top, and white canvas sneakers. She was wearing her glasses as usual, but her red hair, which was always pulled back into a tight ponytail at work, was loose. She squinted at Clara for a moment, as if she had trouble making out who she was.

"Oh, hi," she said. "Do you need something?"

Clara did not like the way she said that, as if Clara were inconsequential, or worse, simply a child.

"I would like to talk to you," Clara said.

"What?" Audrey asked, tilting her ear toward Clara.

Clara repeated herself, something she hated to do, and Audrey replied, "I'm a little busy at the moment. Can you come back later?"

"No."

Audrey sighed, and then stepped aside. "All right. Come in."

The room was fairly large, but it was the only room in the apartment, besides a small bathroom off to the right. To the left, in a nook, was a teeny tiny kitchen, and it was the only modern-looking thing in the apartment. The rest of the room was furnished with what looked to be antiques. There was a tremendous bed, its wooden headboard beautifully carved with leaves and flowers, a pair of chairs whose mahogany legs were carved to look like an animal's claws, and a mahogany vanity. Placed near the room's one window, which faced Washington Square Park, was an elaborately carved rocking chair, its rockers terribly worn, and a sketch pad lying on its seat.

An old fireplace had been boarded up, but its mantel was covered with pencil and charcoal sketches. They all looked somehow similar and yet different. It took Clara a moment to realize that all the drawings were of the view outside the window.

"Did you draw those?" Clara asked.

"What?" Audrey asked.

"I said," Clara repeated in a loud, irritated voice, "DID YOU DRAW THOSE?"

"Yes," Audrey replied.

"They're not very good," Clara said.

"Not very, no," Audrey agreed. There was something very dignified about Audrey, a fact that Clara hadn't noticed before. She didn't like it either. A soup cook should not be dignified.

"Then why do you continue to do it?"

Audrey picked up the sketch pad, placed it on the floor, and sat down heavily in the rocker, as if she were suddenly exhausted. After a minute, she replied, "Have you ever felt that if you focused on something long enough, you would find what you were looking for?"

"On occasion," Clara said, thinking about the times when she tried to recall memories from her childhood.

The sunlight from the window washed across Audrey's face, and Clara looked at her carefully for the first time. Funny, although she'd seen Audrey nearly every day for years, she had never noticed that she had an odd scar that crossed her chin and angled up, like a check mark. Perhaps she'd never noticed because the kitchen lighting was dim, or maybe it was simply that Clara had never bothered to look at Audrey too closely. Yet, now that she did, she noticed something else. This Audrey was made of fine stuff. Her features were smoothly molded, almost aristocratic. Her hands were slender and her neck was long and elegant. Clara thought of her own mother's hands, which were thick and lumpy at the knuckles. She frowned, annoyed at herself for being so distracted. After adjusting her sunglasses and folding her arms across her chest, she asked Audrey what she had come there to find out.

"Tell me how you know Dr. Piff," Clara demanded.

"That's really none of your business," Audrey replied.

Clara felt the blood rush away from her face as fury bloomed in the middle of her chest. For a moment, she was at a loss for words.

"Of course it's my business!" she cried finally. "Everything that happens in the restaurant is my business!"

Audrey did not rise from her seat. Instead, she gazed out the window, rocking slowly in the chair, and calmly replied, "But you are not in the restaurant, Miss Frankofile. You're in my home."

This made Clara so angry that she actually stamped her foot. "I absolutely demand that you tell me how you know Dr. Piff!" She was suddenly, painfully aware of how childishly high-pitched her voice sounded.

"And I absolutely refuse," Audrey said simply.

It was unbelievable to Clara that this soup cook, this Nobody, would speak to her like that, and in a fit of rage she walked over and slapped Audrey across the face. She had never hit anyone before, and it made her palm sting. She looked at her own hand and saw that it was red, and that her fingers were thick and knobby like her mother's. She did not want to look at Audrey, whose skin had felt cold and soft against her hand, but she forced herself to and found that the soup cook was looking at her with something like pity.

Clara's face turned as red as her palm. "You're fired," Clara declared.

For the first time a look of fear passed across Audrey's face, which effectively erased the look of pity. Clara was satisfied.

"Don't bother to come to work tonight. You'll only be

sent away," Clara added before she turned and left the apartment. She stomped down the stairs and threw open the kitchen door so violently that Lila looked up from her reservation book.

"Something wrong?" Lila asked.

"I hate being treated like a child!"

"Who on earth has been treating *you* as a *child?*" Lila asked, genuinely shocked.

"It doesn't matter." Clara shook her head. "The problem is solved."

"Oh, good," sighed Lila, relieved to get back to her reservation book.

That evening, Clara walked into the restaurant feeling lighter and happier than she had since Dr. Piff had left. True, she had not exactly solved the mystery that Dr. Piff had mentioned, but at least she had managed to get rid of Audrey, who (Clara was 98 percent certain) was at the heart of it all.

She sat at her usual table, had her usual meal brought to her, and watched the glittery, fabulous customers. Curiously, the slap she had given Audrey had a strange aftereffect on Clara. She felt a surge of hot, mean energy, and her face, if she had bothered to examine it closely, looked as pink and damp as her father's always did. To be brutally honest, her armpits were giving off a sourish smell, too, not unlike the armpits of her father. But all Clara could smell was imminent success. Tonight she would scout out a Nobody—she could feel it in her bones. And indeed, she had not been in the restaurant for more than fifteen minutes before she spotted her first Nobody. The fake countess, about whom "Ask Ms. Mandy" had just written, appeared at the door, a limp Pekingese tucked beneath her arm. Up front, Lila was looking down at the reservation book, preparing to seat her.

Because Clara was in a strange, mean, buoyant mood, she didn't bother to go quietly to her mother. Instead, she stood up at her table, pointed at the countess, and in her loudest voice declared, "There! That one! She's a Nobody!" She slapped her hand on the table in triumph.

The whole restaurant turned to stare at her, and for a moment she felt a little embarrassed. But not for long. Right after Lila had told the mortified woman to leave, John Sickle, the anchorman who had giggled during the earthquake coverage, entered with several other people.

Oh, this is too easy, Clara thought to herself, her eyes bright as though she had a fever. This time she ran up to the front of the restaurant, knocking her hip painfully against a customer's chair as she went, then jabbed a finger three times at John Sickle's nose. "Nobody, Nobody, Nobody!" she cried, and then smiled at her mother, who looked a little taken aback.

"Are you feeling all right, Clara?" she whispered as John Sickle and his party backed out the front door.

"I'm fine," she said. "Why?"

"You seem a little feverish," Lila said. She put her hand on Clara's forehead. It was a nice feeling, having her mother's hand pressed against her forehead, and Clara closed her eyes, hoping the feeling would last.

"I suppose you're a little warm," Lila said, removing her hand. Clara's forehead felt shivery cold where her mother's hand had been. "Maybe you'd better go home, Clara."

She didn't want to go home, and she didn't really feel sick, except for the strange, jittery, spiteful sensation that she'd had all night. But now that sensation felt tamed, and she suddenly grew a little tired.

"Okay," she said. She hesitated, and almost gave her mother a hug, but Lila had already stuck her head back into the reservation book.

She made her way through the restaurant, aware that some of the customers were looking at her oddly, and went into the kitchen to say good night to her father, who was carefully lifting an entire fried fish out of a pan and onto a plate.

"Good night, Papa."

"Good night already?" he asked without looking up as he spooned some red sauce on the fish.

"Mother says I have a fever," Clara declared. She liked the sound of that and added, in a voice loud enough for the kitchen to hear, "Mother says I should go home immediately and take an aspirin and rest. She'll be in to check on me when she gets home." It was a bit of an exaggeration, but it delighted Clara to say it nevertheless, and she quickly glanced around the kitchen to see if the others had heard. It was then that she saw Audrey, standing in her usual place, ladling soup into a bowl. For a moment Clara was too shocked to say anything.

"Well, then," Pierre was saying, "go home, if you must, but don't talk about fevers in the kitchen, or every single one of these lazy pinheads will suddenly come down with one and—"

"Why are you still here?" Clara interrupted furiously, pointing a finger at Audrey. Audrey did not turn around.

"She don't hear too good," the dishwasher said to Clara.

"But I fired her this morning!" she said angrily to her father.

"Oh, yes, she told me," Pierre said. For once, his voice was quite calm, almost cheerful, as though he were relieved that someone else was doing the yelling in his kitchen.

"Then why is she still here?" Clara demanded, smacking her hand on the metal pick-up counter, making the dishes that were lined up on the shelf clatter loudly.

"Because the woman makes a damn fine soup," he replied. It was the first kind word he had ever said about an employee, and the entire kitchen staff now stopped what they were doing to stare at him in disbelief. In the uncharacteristic silence, Pierre's face suddenly collapsed into a livid scowl.

"Who said you could stop working, you putrid heap of bat droppings . . ."

His booming voice drowned out Clara's protests. Furious and mortified, she looked at Audrey, who had finally glanced up from her pot. Behind her thick glasses, her eyes met with Clara's. They were proud eyes, the sort of eyes a soup cook had no business having.

She thinks she's won, thought Clara. She hasn't. She's hiding something, and I won't have things hidden from me.

I'll find out her secret. She has no idea how far I'm willing to take this.

Clara, in truth, didn't exactly know herself how far that might be. But as she walked home, the night air skimming across her feverish skin and cooling it, she considered that it might be pretty far indeed.

CHAPTER TEN

D r. Piff had an office in a very sleek high-rise building across the street from Central Park. Outside the building was a massive red metal sculpture of the office building's numbers—464—each number twice as tall as Clara.

Clara did not relish the idea of seeing Dr. Piff again. Once she declared someone a Nobody, it was generally unpleasant to see them again. But it seemed to her that she had no choice now. She took the elevator to the sixteenth floor and walked into Dr. Piff's big, fancy waiting room. It was completely empty, except for a receptionist who smiled at Clara with a confused look on her face.

"Can I help you?" she asked pleasantly.

"I'm here to see Dr. Piff."

The receptionist's face fell, and she blinked rapidly three or four times.

"And . . . how do you know him?" she asked, in an overly polite voice.

Clara paused, then said, "He's a friend."

"Oh." She looked at Clara for a moment, nodding. She

picked up the phone, dialed an extension, and said, "Would you please come to the reception desk for a moment?"

Clara sat down on the couch and waited, flipping through some old magazines. Inside one was a large photo of the melancholy actress June Loblolly, and above her picture was the heading "Doom and Gloom June." This was the very article, in fact, that had turned June Loblolly into a Nobody. Sometimes it happened that way. An article would appear in a magazine or a newspaper, and all of a sudden everyone was talking about it. And everyone had talked about this article. In a matter of days, the nickname Doom and Gloom June had stuck.

Clara looked at June Loblolly's photo. It was not so much that she had a sad look on her face, but that her features were strangely set, so that she always gave the *appearance* of being gloomy.

Finally, a tall, handsome, auburn-haired woman appeared at the reception desk, and the receptionist said to her, "Ah, Ms. Piff! This young lady is asking for your father. She says she's a friend of his."

Ms. Piff looked at Clara with her auburn eyebrows arched high. Clara had heard Dr. Piff speak about his daughter, but she had always got the feeling that he didn't like her very much.

"Come this way, please," Ms. Piff said to Clara. She turned, and her heels clicked down the hallway and into an office with a large desk in the center covered with papers, and behind the desk were three file cabinets that were all open and empty. On the floor were a dozen or so cartons.

"Sit down, please," said Ms. Piff coolly, gesturing for Clara to sit down on a little chair while she went around and sat behind the desk. "Now, what is this about?"

"Where's Dr. Piff?" Clara asked.

"Dr. Piff is dead," she said. Then, seeing the shock on Clara's face, she added, "I'm sorry to be so blunt, but I believe in being direct in such matters, even with children."

"How?" Clara managed to murmur.

"A heart attack. Just yesterday." She stiffened when she saw the look on Clara's face, and added, "If you are going to cry, I can provide you with tissues, or I can put my arm around you. Which would you prefer?"

"I'm not going to cry."

"That's good." Ms. Piff seemed to relax a little.

In fact, Clara felt a little numb. She had never known anyone who had died.

"Is there anything else I can do for you?" Ms. Piff asked in a way that really meant "Now it's time for you to leave."

Clara hesitated, having forgotten momentarily why she had come. "No," she said absently, and she rose to leave. But then she stopped and said, "Yes. Yes, I have a question about someone. I think she was a patient of Dr. Piff's. Her name is Audrey—"

"Oh, for goodness' sake, don't talk to me about my father's patients!" Ms. Piff had clearly used up all the compassion she had in reserve, and now her tone was downright snappish. "Look around." She indicated the boxes scattered all over the floor, each marked with letters on the lids, like A-D, and E-G. "I've been knee deep in my father's patients all morning—hundreds of them. Good Lord, he was a terrible slob."

Clara winced. It bothered her somehow to hear Dr. Piff described in those terms.

"Now, if that's all . . ." Ms. Piff clapped her knees and stood up. She'd apparently had enough of chatting with an eleven-year-old girl.

"I think perhaps I *am* going to cry," said Clara. "Would you please get me a tissue?"

Ms. Piff sighed very loudly. "You might have cried before, you know, when I first made the offer."

"It's just coming on now," Clara said.

"Oh, fine." And Ms. Piff and her clicking heels left the room.

Clara knelt beside the *A–D* file box and thumbed through the files quickly. No sign of a file for Audrey Aster.

She stood up, sighed, lifted her sunglasses, and propped them up on her head. Then she saw it. It was lying on top of a pile of papers and magazines on the floor near the window: a beautifully framed drawing of a goldfish swimming in a lopsided fishbowl. The goldfish was wearing blue pants, and was smiling. There were braces on its teeth. In the bottom left-hand corner was her own childish, printed signature.

Oh! She remembered that drawing! She had made it for Dr. Piff when she was six. She remembered drawing it, too, and how she'd labored over the tiny braces. Now she crouched down, staring at it in wonder. It was like finding an ancient relic that had been buried in the earth, forgotten and waiting to be discovered again. *And she did remember it!* It was a small thing to remember, especially when she had forgotten so many other things about her childhood, but it thrilled her anyway.

At the sound of the click-clicking of Ms. Piff's heels, she grabbed the framed picture, upsetting the pile beneath it. It toppled and splayed, and there, underneath an issue of *Modern Optics* magazine, was a thick manila envelope, its flap tied closed by a frayed string coiled around a round cardboard clasp. The envelope seemed quite old. It was soft and pulpy, and so stuffed that there was a long tear along the bottom edge, out of which poked a piece of paper. Clara could see only two fragments of sentences, handwritten with blue ink: . . . *but Audrey does not respond.* And on the following line, . . . *from Pish Posh. That would be the worst possible thing I can imagine!*

"What are you doing?" Ms. Piff asked suspiciously, entering the room with a box of tissues in her hand. Clara straightened up quickly.

"This is mine," she said, clutching the goldfish picture tightly to her chest. "I drew it for Dr. Piff."

"That thing? Take it, I don't mind. It was in the garbage pile anyway." She indicated the mess of papers on the floor.

"You were going to throw it away?" Clara cried.

"We can't keep all my father's junk, you know." Then, seeing that she'd offended Clara, she added, "Well, for heaven's sake, he had the thing up on his wall for years! That should make you happy."

It didn't. In fact, it made Clara miserable. She felt ensnared in a horrible tangle of guilt and sorrow. She'd banished Dr. Piff from Pish Posh, and he'd died right afterward. And he had kept her picture up on his office wall for so many years. How must he have felt that night when she told him he was a Nobody? Clara's eyes grew hot, and a strange, thick sensation in her throat made her press her tongue against the roof of her mouth.

Clara tried to remember when she first met Dr. Piff, but couldn't. He just always seemed to be standing on the edge of her life—calm and quiet, and watching her with his small, intelligent eyes. Now he was dead. He was not a Somebody or a Nobody anymore. He was simply gone.

"So, do you need these?" Ms. Piff asked impatiently, holding the box of tissues out toward Clara.

Clara took a deep breath. No, she was not going to cry. Decidedly not. Absolutely not. She shook her head.

"No?" Ms. Piff said. "Well, I wish you'd make up your mind. Okay, then"—she gave Clara's back a little nudge with the tips of her fingers—"off you go."

Clara sidestepped away from Ms. Piff, knelt down quickly, and went to grab the old envelope. But before she could pick it up, Ms. Piff's hard black heel clamped down on the file.

"I don't believe that belongs to you," she said.

"It's going to be thrown out anyway," Clara protested. "You said this is the garbage pile."

"The garbage pile, not the free-to-a-good-home pile," Ms. Piff replied tartly. She pinched her fingers into Clara's shoulder until Clara stood, and then all but shoved Clara out the door. But before she left, Clara whirled around.

"Dr. Piff was *not* a slob!" she cried, making Ms. Piff's

auburn eyebrows rise nearly to her hairline. "He stacked his plates for the busboys. And his hair was always neatly combed!" It was a weak defense of Dr. Piff, and she knew it. So did Ms. Piff, who dismissed her outburst by shutting the office door in Clara's face.

Clara turned and walked back down the hall, feeling furious with Ms. Piff but even more furious with herself. She'd had her hand right on the envelope, which contained—she was certain—the answer to Audrey's secret. Now the envelope would be thrown out. Audrey the soup cook had won.

Suddenly, a thought occurred to her, one that she had not bothered wondering about before. Why had Dr. Piff mentioned the "most peculiar and mysterious thing" if he had not wanted her to figure out what it was? Surely he knew that she would insist upon finding out what it was. Had he deliberately sent her on a quest? Yes, now that she thought of it, she was almost certain that he had.

She felt her muscles tighten and her spine draw up. Lifting her glasses off the top of her head, she replaced them on her nose. The world dimmed through the dark lenses, and as she nibbled on the ends of her hair, her brain began to churn. She was determined that she would not let Dr. Piff down again. And when she was determined to do a certain thing, that thing was as good as done.

CHAPTER ELEVEN

It took Clara exactly three and a half minutes to figure out what she needed to do next. Outside Dr. Piff's office, she fetched a cab, and a few minutes later she was on Annabelle's doorstep, pressing the doorbell.

It was Annabelle's father, Mr. Arbutnot, who came to the door. His pleasant face looked distressed, but when he saw it was Clara, his expression brightened instantly.

"Annabelle's friend, isn't it?" He ushered her in immediately and beckoned her to follow him upstairs, explaining as they went, "Annabelle locked herself in her room yesterday, and she won't speak to me at all, or even open her door."

"What's wrong with her?" Clara asked.

"Oh, let's just say she's never handled change very well."

At the top of the stairs, he turned down a short hallway, and knocked on the first door to the left. There was no answer.

"Annabelle? Honey? Your friend—" He paused here and whispered to Clara, "I don't think I know your name." She told him, and he called through the door, "—your friend Clara is here to see you."

There was silence at first, then, "Tell her I'm sick."

"You don't *sound* sick," Clara shot back. Silence again. Then, in another minute, the door opened a crack. Mr. Arbutnot gave Clara a soft, encouraging pat on her back and left her.

"I'm not in the mood for company," Annabelle said squarely, then started to close the door. But Clara wedged her foot in the opening.

"I didn't come here to give you any," Clara said.

"I already returned your pearls," Annabelle said glumly. "What more do you want?"

"I'll tell you if you let me in." With a quick shove, Clara pushed open the door, sending Annabelle backward a few steps. Annabelle's room was a mess, with crumpled clothing strewn across the floor and a spill of magazines beside her bed. But Annabelle herself was in even worse shape. She was dressed in a pair of wrinkled flannel pajamas, and her hair was sticking out every which way.

"When's the last time you combed your hair?" Clara asked. Annabelle scowled and hastily ran a hand through her disheveled hair. Then she turned her back to Clara and sat down on her bed.

"What's the matter with you, anyway?" Clara asked, folding her arms across her chest.

Annabelle turned around, and Clara noticed that her eyes were red-rimmed and puffy, as though she'd been crying.

"Everything."

If anyone else had said this, Clara would have dismissed

them as being overdramatic, but there was a truly desperate tone to Annabelle's voice.

"What happened?" Clara asked.

"My father has decided to go legit. No more burglarizing. No more jewelry heists. He's going to be a full-time hypnotherapist! And I'm supposed to be a full-time normal kid. I'll have to do things like join the school chorus and have slumber parties and worry about which lip gloss to wear . . . oh, cripes, can you even *picture* it?" she wailed. In truth, Clara could not picture it. Then she remembered why she had come in the first place . . . and suddenly she felt just as rotten as Annabelle.

"That's bad. Bad for both of us."

"Why for both of us?" Annabelle asked.

"Because I came here to hire you and your father to steal something for me."

"Really?" Annabelle perked up at this, and her eyes suddenly looked a little less mournful. "Steal what?"

"Nothing valuable," Clara said a little cagily, suddenly aware that she didn't want to tell Annabelle everything. "Just a manila envelope from a doctor's office."

"A doctor's office, huh? Okay, okay . . ." Annabelle was out of bed now, heading for her desk and looking, miraculously, fully recovered. "What's the address?"

"What does it matter?" Clara shrugged. "Your father won't do it."

"That doesn't mean *I* can't."

Clara toyed with this new idea. Could Annabelle do it on her own?

"Your father would kill you," Clara suggested.

"Not if he doesn't know. Now come on, what's the address?"

Clara told her, and Annabelle immediately sat down at her desk and booted up her computer.

"What are you doing?" Clara asked.

"Pull up a chair. I'll show you."

Annabelle logged on to the Internet and plunked in a Web site address. On the screen, a Web site popped up: The American Association of Burglars, Crooks, and Ne'er-Do-Wells. In the corner of the screen was an animation of a man with dark beard stubble and a black mask across his eyes, who kept putting one finger to his lips and saying, "Shhhhhh."

"You have to be a member," Annabelle explained as she entered a password. "It costs a heap of money, but they have a great database."

Annabelle's password was accepted, and the screen changed to a search engine. This time the animation of the grizzled burglar winked through his mask. Annabelle typed in the address of Dr. Piff's office, and immediately a photo of a high-rise building appeared on-screen.

"That's Dr. Piff's office building!" Clara exclaimed, and no sooner had she spoken than the image changed to a three-dimensional drawing of the high-rise, which turned around and around, so that you could see every angle, with all the floors visible. Little coins of different colors flashed in different parts of the building—green, silver, and gold.

"What do the coins mean?" Clara asked.

"Oh, they just tell you which offices have anything worth

stealing. Green means there's some stuff worth taking, but nothing to write home about. Silver is better, and gold means you've hit the jackpot. But see what's inside some of the coins?"

Clara leaned in closer to the computer screen. In some of the coins was a pair of tiny handcuffs.

"What's that supposed to mean?" she asked Annabelle.

"That means the office has high security . . . you know, laser beams, high-tech alarm systems—a real nightmare for burglars."

"Well, what about Dr. Piff's office?"

"What floor is he on?"

"The sixteenth. Office number sixteen seventy-one."

Annabelle typed in this information, and the sixteenth floor appeared on the screen, with all its flashing coins.

"We're in luck." Annabelle pointed to the door marked 1671, where a green coin was flashing steadily. "Light security." Annabelle clicked on the green coin, and then clicked the burglar's nose for more information.

"Easy pickings," the masked burglar icon growled, "if youse got a thing for stethoscopes and tongue depressors."

"There's a single alarm," Annabelle said, "which I can disarm, no problem."

"Good." Clara sat back in the chair, satisfied. "Then this will be easy."

"Hardly." Annabelle bit at her lower lip, then clicked back to the floor plan of the entire building. "You see, we have to get into the building first, and that's going to be the challenge. We'll have to enter through the front door, and there's a security guard stationed there twenty-four hours a day."

"Oh." Clara slumped back in her chair and sighed. "Then it's hopeless."

"Cripes, you give up easily," Annabelle said.

Clara looked at Annabelle, beginning to get irritated. "All I want to know is whether you can do it or not."

"And all I'm saying is there's always a loophole. Well, almost always. See the ice-cream cone?" She moved the cursor to a tiny icon of a chocolate ice-cream cone in the upper left-hand corner of the screen. "That's a feature called the Inside Scoop. Frankly, it's why most of us burglars are willing to pay so much money to become a member of the American Association of Burglars, Crooks, and Ne'er-Do-Wells. Watch this." Annabelle clicked on the ice-cream cone, and on the monitor a movie started to play. The movie showed a pale man with a thin, hard face and massive shoulders sitting behind a desk in the lobby of Dr. Piff's office building. The man's body was very, very still, but his eyes were constantly moving between several security monitors that sat on his desk. He put out a finger and touched a button on one of the monitors. Then he reached into the inside pocket of his jacket and pulled out a small rectangular packet, which he quickly tore open. He pulled something out of the packet and began to rub it on his hands.

"Dis here is Stan Heckle, da nighttime security guard." The masked bandit icon was narrating the film—you could see his lips moving. "Don't let his pasty-faced mug fool youse. He's a tough customer—smart and mean as sin. In fact, da guy used to be a burglar hisself, in London, till he reformed and became a security guard. He knows all da tricks, and dat makes him dangerous. Also, when Stan catches a burglar, he don't call the police. He takes da matter into his own hands. Like what he did to da burglar last month, for instance . . ."

There was a pause, while the icon's thick black eyebrows rose with significance.

"Well?" Clara turned to Annabelle. "Isn't he going to tell us what happened?"

Annabelle whispered back. "He wants us to ask him what happened. Go ahead. Type it in. But sound like you're very interested."

"I *am* very interested!" Clara replied.

What did he do to the burglar last month? Clara typed the question into the little question box on the upper right-hand corner of the screen. Annabelle stuck her elbow into Clara's side, and Clara added, *I'm dying to know.* She pressed ENTER.

"Are youse sure you want to hear?" the masked burglar asked coyly.

"He's milking this one . . . it must be good," Annabelle said. She leaned across Clara and typed, *We're on pins and needles! We're frothing at the mouth with anticipation!!!* then pressed ENTER.

"Calm down, will youse! Okay, here's what happened. Last month Stan caught a burglar in da building. Stan tied da poor guy up, put a gag over his mouth, shoved him in da building's mail pouch, and took him home. Da guy ain't been seen since den. But I'll tell youse what. One month later a body washed up on da banks of da Hudson River, and da burglar's wife said she was eighty-eight percent sure it was her husband. She couldn't be a hundred percent certain, see, since he didn't have a head no more."

Clara blanched and looked at Annabelle, but Annabelle's eyes were focused on Stan.

"Stan's got one weakness, though," the burglar continued. "He's terrified of germs. Hates to touch t'ings dat other people touch. Dat's why he washes his hands constantly wit dem Handi Wipes in his pocket." Even now, on-screen, Stan Heckle had pulled out another packet of Handi Wipes from his jacket.

The screen changed again, and a tall, well-built woman with a gigantic floppy hat walked into the lobby.

"Da dame is Alexandra Von Bolsterboggin. Vavava-voom!" the masked burglar exclaimed. "Now, here's where t'ings get inneresting. Dere's a doctor in dis building—Dr. Muster on da tenth floor. He fixes up ladies' faces—you know, injecting gunk into dere wrinkles, changing da shape of dere noses or lips. Sometimes he changes da faces so much, ya can't even recognize dem afterward . . . crazy dames! But here's da t'ing: he works only on rich and famous dames, da kind youse read about in da papers. And because dey don't want people to know who dey are, dey come in da evening, so's da tabloids don't get wind of it."

The screen showed Alexandra Von Bolsterboggin walking up to Stan at the security desk. She said something to Stan, and he picked up a phone while Alexandra drummed her manicured fingers nervously on his desk.

"Stan's dialing Dr. Muster on da office intercom, just to check and see if da dame is really expected in his office," the masked burglar explained. "If da doctor says she ain't, Stan will have no problem with tossing her over his shoulder and giving her da heave-ho, headfirst, right onto da sidewalk."

Stan put the phone down and nodded shortly to Alexandra, who rushed to the elevators. The second she left, Stan took out a spray bottle of cleaning solution and a rag, and began to spray and scrub at the spot on his desk where Alexandra's fingers had been tapping.

"Okay, so the security guard has a phobia about germs and some lady is going to get rid of her wrinkles." Clara shook her head, perplexed. "So what?"

"Shaa!" Annabelle snapped back. "I'm thinking." She slumped down in her chair and stared hard at the monitor, gnawing at the edge of her thumb. She sat like that for so long that Clara had to resist the urge to nudge her. Finally, she sat up straight and began to type, *Can you give me Dr. Muster's patient schedule for tonight?*

"Now you're t'inking!" the masked burglar said. "Tonight, Dr. Muster has a patient due in for major face surgery at eight o'clock. I mean *major!* She's having her nose bobbed, her lips poufed, her cheekbones cheekier. Her own mudder won't recognize her after da doc is finished wit her. She must be pretty important, 'cause I can't get her real name. Da doctor's database lists this dame only as Patient X. Now, you want my opinion on how to do dis job?"

Yes, please, Annabelle typed in.

"Youse show up at seven forty-five, dressed like some

dame who don't want to be recognized—you know, big hat, large sunglasses, a scarf. And youse tell Stan dat you are Patient X, come for your appointment. If youse come any earlier than dat, Stan might get suspicious. Dat means youse got only fifteen minutes to do da job, because once da real Patient X shows up, Stan is going to flip on every stinkin' alarm in da building and da cops will be there in five minutes. Got it? Any questions?"

Annabelle typed in, *What if Patient X is early for her appointment?*

It took a moment, and then the masked burglar said, "Youse have a second person waiting outside. If a car pulls up and a dame gets out, dat second person will have to find a way to persuade her not to go into da building—for example, a good knock on the noggin usually does da job. Any other questions?"

Clara leaned forward and typed in, *What are the chances that this will work?*

In a minute, the masked burglar said, "Slim to none."

Clara's face fell. "Slim to none?" she said to Annabelle. "That doesn't sound very promising."

"That's because you're not a burglar," Annabelle replied.

CHAPTER TWELVE

Annabelle sat at the computer, scrolling through all sorts of information—lists of people, a map of the surrounding neighborhood, parties and conventions and concerts that were happening that evening, and all kinds of other stuff.

"Is this all necessary?" Clara groaned after an hour of watching Annabelle tap away at the mouse.

"Oh, no, not at all. In fact, if you ask most burglars, they'll tell you that they don't do any research at all. Oh—but you *can't* ask them, can you . . . because the burglars who don't do any research are all in JAIL!" She glared at Clara and went back to work.

Annabelle sat at the computer for so long that Clara's stomach started growling.

"Oh, go downstairs and eat something, will you?" Annabelle snapped. "I can't think with your internal organs rattling away like maracas!"

Clara was too embarrassed to be angry, but she did mutter something about *foul moods* and *anal-retentive burglars* before she left the room.

After searching through the Arbutnots' refrigerator and cupboards for tomato juice or tuna fish and finding only odd, unidentifiable foods that were either brown or green, she settled on a package of mossy brownish-green cubes of something called Spirulina Treats. The package said they were a delicious phytonutrient-rich snack, sweetened with a touch of honey. At least they were sweet. Clara took the package and returned to Annabelle's room.

"Finished?" Clara asked hopefully as she ripped open the package of Spirulina Treats.

"With the research," Annabelle said. "Next is the equipment." She seemed more relaxed now, however.

"Oh, Spirulina Treats!" she said, noticing the package in Clara's hand. "Toss one over here."

Clara did, and then bit into hers. It tasted like the gunk you'd scrape off the bottom of a pond. Sweetened with a touch of honey.

"They're really good for your immune system," Annabelle said encouragingly, seeing the face Clara was making.

"They *taste* like they're good for your immune system."

She and Annabelle spent the rest of the day finalizing their plans and gathering equipment, most of which was tucked away in neat black leather cases stowed in Annabelle's closet: lock picks, computerized alarm disarmers, ropes for climbing ("Just in case," Annabelle had said, and Clara got the distinct impression that Annabelle was *hoping* she'd have to scale the building). Finally, Annabelle tried on her Patient X disguise: a conservative navy blue dress, black high heels, and a big hat, the brim of which flopped down low over her face. Then she rolled a tube of red lipstick across her lips and straightened her usual tall-girl slump.

"How do I look?" Annabelle asked, smiling and spreading her arms wide.

"Don't smile. And make your voice deeper."

"How do I look?" Annabelle said in a lower voice.

Clara studied her. What with the outfit and her height, Annabelle could probably pass—probably.

"Not bad," Clara said. "But put these on, too, just in case." Clara removed her sunglasses and handed them to Annabelle, but Annabelle waved them away.

"I've got my own pair," Annabelle explained. She rummaged through her closet, brought out a small leather case the size of a dictionary, and placed it on her bed. Inside, nestled carefully in pale blue silk lining, were two pairs of large, homely, black sunglasses.

"Mine are much nicer," Clara said frankly.

"You think so? Here." Annabelle handed Clara a pair. "Try these on."

Clara held the glasses by one stem, and sneered, "They look like something you'd buy at the drugstore."

"Oh, don't be such a snob," Annabelle said. She took them and put them on Clara's face. Then she put the other pair on herself.

"I'll be right back," Annabelle said. She turned and left

the room, and Clara could hear her feet clomping down the stairs.

Clara got up and looked at herself in the mirror. The glasses were horrible—the completely wrong shape for her face, and so cheap looking. I'm *not* a snob, she thought defensively. It's just that I know the difference between tasteful and tacky.

She reached up to remove the glasses when she heard a voice—Annabelle's voice—very distinctly in her ear: "So . . . do you still think your glasses are nicer?"

Clara turned around, but the room was empty and the door was shut. Was she hearing things?

"I asked you a question, Clara." Annabelle's voice was in her ear again. "Do you still think your—"

The glasses! Clara whipped them off and examined them. Right by the bend at the stem was a cluster of pinprick holes shaped in a circle, like a miniature telephone receiver. On the other stem, in the same spot, was a raised black button with a single hole in the center. Clara raised the button to her lips and whistled loudly into it.

"Ow!" She heard Annabelle's muffled cry from the glasses' receiving end.

Placing the glasses back on, Clara heard Annabelle complaining, "— was a crappy thing to do! Are you trying to make me deaf?"

"What are these things?" Clara asked.

"They're called Spyfocals. My dad gave them to me for my birthday last year. What do you think of them?"

"I think they're just a fancy version of walkie-talkies."

There was utter silence on the other end. Clearly, Clara had offended Annabelle.

"Annabelle?" Clara said. No answer. Who would have guessed she'd be so sensitive? Clara thought, shaking her head.

And then, amazingly, Clara found herself looking into a tiny movie screen—actually two movie screens that combined as one—on the inside lenses of her glasses. She was watching a film of Annabelle's house. The image kept changing, as if the camera were moving down Annabelle's hallway, until it stopped in front of Mr. Arbutnot's office. A fist shot out on the screen and knocked on the door.

"Come in." Clara could hear Mr. Arbutnot's voice, and the office door opened. Now Clara realized what she was watching.

There must be a camera in the glasses, and I'm watching things through Annabelle's eyes, she thought.

On the screen Mr. Arbutnot looked up from his desk and smiled when he saw Annabelle.

"Feeling better?" he asked.

"A little."

"Your friend cheered you up, then?"

"Who, Clara? Nah. She's in no shape to cheer anybody up."

"Really? What's the matter with her?"

"Well . . . you promise you won't tell anyone?" Annabelle said.

"Of course not."

What is she doing!? Clara thought. She's going to give away the whole thing!

"Foot fungus. Oh, it's awful. Turns her toenails brown, and the smell . . ."

"Annabelle!" Clara cried.

"Isn't there something the doctors can do about it?" Mr. Arbutnot asked.

"They've tried everything—antibiotic creams, footbaths. Nothing seems to work."

"Poor kid."

"I helped her paint her toenails red. You know . . . so the fungus doesn't show as much."

"You're a good friend, Annabelle."

"I hate you, Annabelle," Clara hissed, her face crimson.

"Well, I'm glad to see that you are up and about, in any case." Mr. Arbutnot smiled at his daughter, then tilted his head. "But why are you wearing the Spyfocals?"

"Oh. I just thought . . . since I won't be using them anymore for jobs . . . I guess I was feeling a little sentimental."

"Don't worry, Annabelle. Once you start getting involved with school and friends, you won't even miss burgling houses. It will be a fresh start for both of us."

"Sure, Dad. Hey, Clara asked if I can go over to her parents' restaurant for dinner tonight."

"Okay, I guess that's fine. But sweetheart?"

"Yeah?"

"You're still a little young for lipstick, don't you think?"

"Oh. Sure, Dad. I was just messing around. Well, I guess

I better get back upstairs. The nail polish is probably dry by now. If only I could help her with the odor . . ."

Then the screen in Clara's glasses went blank, and she was looking out through the lenses once again. In another minute came the sound of feet clomping up the stairs. The door opened and Annabelle walked in. She removed her Spyfocals and grinned.

"Foot fungus?" Clara said angrily.

"Oh, relax. My dad won't tell anyone."

"But I don't *have* foot fungus!"

"You still think Spyfocals are just fancy walkie-talkies?"

"No," Clara grudgingly admitted, taking them off and handing them back to Annabelle.

"Hang on to them," Annabelle said lightly.

"What for?"

"Well, we'll have to have some way of communicating while we're on the job."

"*We?*" Clara shook her head. "No, not we. I'm hiring *you* to do this."

"First of all, I'm not taking your money," Annabelle said.

"You had no trouble taking my jewelry," Clara grumbled.

"Second of all," Annabelle continued, ignoring her remark, "I need another person to watch for Patient X."

"Then *find* another person. Another professional," Clara said.

"Rule number one in burgling: the more people you involve in a job, the more likely the job will get all botched up." Annabelle's face had turned very serious now, and her dark eyes bore down on Clara's. "If you want to get your envelope from this doctor's office, then we do this job together. Otherwise"—Annabelle laid her Spyfocals carefully and deliberately in their silk-lined case—"find yourself another burglar."

Clara glared at Annabelle for a minute. "I am not a thief," she said arrogantly.

"Fine," Annabelle said crisply, and she held out her hand. "Give me the glasses, and this whole conversation never even happened. Poof. It's gone from my brain."

Clara handed back the glasses, which Annabelle tucked into the box. Then Annabelle collapsed back onto her bed and shut her eyes, as if Clara had already left.

Dropping the whole thing was the most sensible thing to do, Clara thought. But then she began to think of Dr. Piff. She had sworn to herself that she would not disappoint him again. Plus, to be perfectly honest, she couldn't bear the thought of spending night after night in Pish Posh, knowing that something peculiar was going on right under her nose. And that a soup cook had succeeded in defying her.

"Okay," Clara said.

"Okay what?"

"Okay, I'll stand outside and watch for Patient X. But what do I tell her if she comes early?"

Annabelle sat up again and looked Clara up and down. "Well, you're a lot shorter than me, but we can roll up the pants."

"What pants?" said Clara. "I don't wear pants."

"Ooh, and I have the perfect top," Annabelle continued, ignoring Clara.

"Perfect for what?"

"Have you ever been to Sandusky, Ohio?" Annabelle asked.

"Of course not!"

"Well, tonight you are Emily McBickle, lead soprano in the Sandusky, Ohio, Girls' Choir. And silly you! You got separated from your group and are all alone and lost in New York City."

"Is that what I'm supposed to tell Patient X?" Clara guessed.

"With tears in your eyes."

"I don't cry."

"Practice."

For the next hour, Clara thought of all sorts of sad things—her parents dying, herself dying, Pish Posh closing down—but all she could manage was a weak squealing sound, which made her sound like a dolphin, and she couldn't manage to work up any tears.

"Forget it. You might pop a blood vessel," Annabelle said finally, rolling her eyes. "Just try not to look so superior."

CHAPTER THIRTEEN

As it turned out, it was quite easy for Clara to not look so superior: she was dressed in a pair of cheap stonewashed jeans that were rolled up three times at the cuff and a perfectly hideous lime-green shirt with a giant panda-bear head appliquéd on. The panda's eyes were made of huge clear-plastic bubbles, which contained little black balls for pupils that bobbled around crazily as Clara walked. On her feet she wore a pair of Annabelle's old sneakers.

Annabelle was dressed as Patient X, with a large designer tote bag slung over her shoulder containing burglary equipment, including the Spyfocals.

On the street, Clara's hand automatically shot out to hail a cab, but Annabelle grabbed her by the wrist and pulled her hand down.

"No cabs. We're going by subway," Annabelle said, and she began walking east at a brisk pace.

"The subway?"

"Of course."

"*You* can go by subway, if you want. I'm going by cab,"

Clara said firmly. In truth, Clara had never been on a subway. According to everything she had heard, they were filthy and dangerous, and to be avoided at all cost.

"No, you're not," Annabelle replied just as firmly. "The idea is to be inconspicuous. Cabdrivers are nosy. On a train, people don't look at each other. In fact, it's practically a rule that they don't look at each other. We're going by subway." And she picked up her pace, not even bothering to look back and see if Clara was following her.

The sneakers were not at all what Clara had expected. Her feet had never felt so close to the ground, yet they were delightfully cushioned and so bouncy that she had a strange urge to run, and a few times she deliberately let Annabelle get ahead of her in order to launch herself into a springy jog to catch up. At the subway station, as they descended the long flight of stairs, Clara covered her nose.

"I smell urine," she complained.

Annabelle gave her a sidelong look. "Subway stairs always smell like that."

Clara breathed through her mouth until they reached the bottom, where there was a large booth and several turnstiles, past which was a concrete platform.

"Here." Annabelle pressed a thin paper card in Clara's hand.

"What's this for?"

"What's it *for*?" Annabelle asked incredulously. "It gets you into the subway. You swipe it at the turnstile." She gazed at Clara curiously for a minute, and then said, "Cripes, you've never been on the subway before, have you?"

"You have lipstick on your teeth," Clara said diffidently.

Annabelle rubbed at her teeth with the edge of her thumb. "I've never heard of someone who grew up in New York and has never—"

"It's seven thirty-five, Annabelle."

"Okay. Just swipe the card through the slot there. That's it. And just push through the turnstile—harder. There you go."

On the subway platform was a smattering of people milling around. They were very average looking. Nobody seemed particularly dangerous. The urine smell was gone, replaced by a dry, hot, tinny odor, which grew even stronger when the train thundered into the station. The noise grew so loud that Clara took a few steps back in alarm, but Annabelle grabbed her by the arm and practically shoved her through the train's doors when they slid open.

Before Clara sat down, she examined the molded plastic seat for filth. It looked clean enough, but she brushed it off just in case. The door slid closed with a *shoosh* and the train lurched into motion. Just as Annabelle had said, the other passengers didn't look at each other, but stared straight ahead, out the window. Their eyes jiggered back and forth, like the panda's eyes on her T-shirt.

"It's not so bad—the subway," Clara said after a few minutes.

Annabelle slid her eyes toward Clara and shook her head. "You're a strange duck."

They rode the rest of the way in silence and got off at the

Seventy-ninth Street station. The stairs at that station smelled of urine, too. When they reached street level, Clara could see Dr. Piff's office building directly across the street. That was when she felt the first pang of nervousness. It was one thing to plot out a robbery from a computer screen, but it was quite another to actually do it.

"Wait." Clara grabbed Annabelle's arm as she started for the office building.

"For what?"

"Maybe we shouldn't."

"You've just got the jitters. That'll pass. Let's go." But before she could take another step, Clara grabbed her arm again.

"*What?!*" Annabelle snapped. "Clara, it is seven forty-four. If we are going to do this, we have to do it now. Do you want that envelope?"

"Yes," Clara said almost inaudibly. And she did.

"Okay then." And they both walked across the street to 464 Fifth Avenue. Annabelle took the Spyfocals out of her bag. She put hers on and handed the other pair to Clara, then took one long, last appraising look at her.

"Okay, who are you?" Annabelle asked.

"Emily McBickle, lead soprano in the Sandusky, Ohio, Girls' Choir."

"Fabulous. Now tuck yourself into the six," Annabelle said.

"What?"

"The six." Annabelle pointed to the 6 in the metal 464

sculpture. Clara went to the sculpture, ducked her head, and curled herself up into the hole of the 6, wedging herself in snugly.

"Ready?" Annabelle said. Clara nodded.

"Be careful, Annabelle."

She watched as Annabelle walked to the building and disappeared inside. Through her Spyfocals Clara could hear the sound of Annabelle's heels clicking against the marble floor, and then the soft thump of a heavy door closing behind her.

"Who are you here to see?" Annabelle heard a man's voice ask. He had a strong British accent, so she knew he must be Stan Heckle.

"Dr. Muster. I have an appointment at eight," she heard Annabelle reply. Good—she had lowered her voice to sound older.

"Your name?"

"Patient X," Annabelle said. There was a pause, during which Clara held her breath, straining to hear what was happening. Had Stan Heckle looked at Annabelle and realized that she was too young to be Patient X? Clara's muscles contracted, and she felt a subtle tremor course through them.

In a moment, she heard Stan say, "Hello, Dr. Muster. I have a Patient X in the lobby. She says she has an appointment with you." He sounded as if he really didn't believe that she did, but apparently Dr. Muster confirmed it, because there was a soft click and then Stan said to Annabelle, "All right, then. You can go on up."

So that was that. She was in. Clara's muscles began to relax. Now all she had to do was wait and keep a sharp lookout in case Patient X decided to arrive early.

The streets were nearly empty in this part of the city. In the strange evening hush, she began to think about Pish Posh. She wondered what people had thought that night, seeing the empty little round table at the back. She suspected that they would be relieved to see that she was not there. In her mind she could hear them chattering gaily; no one would be nervous about being kicked out, no one would wonder if they were becoming a Nobody. The image was so clear: Pish Posh would be a much happier place without Clara in it. They didn't see that it was *she* who made sure that the restaurant remained special. If she let everyone stay, Pish Posh would be no different than any other restaurant in New York.

Curled up in the 6, Clara felt a nasty pang of self-pity. It expanded by degrees, and she imagined herself being caught by Stan Heckle and being bundled up in a mailbag and taken to the Hudson River, where she would be strangled, and then be found (headless!) by some man walking his dog. And even though she didn't have a head, Annabelle would be able to identify her from the panda-bear shirt, and it would be in all the newspapers (both the fact that she was dead *and* that she was wearing bad clothing). But no one would come to her funeral, not even her parents, because they would be too busy at Pish Posh, and as her small, expensive casket was being lowered into the ground—

"Clara!" a voice called in her ear, and she jumped and hit

her head on the top of the 6's hole. "I'm on the sixteenth floor, right outside Piff's office." The screen on the glasses came on, and Clara could see the door with the nameplate inscribed with Dr. Piff's name. A hand suddenly obscured the view and waved at her—Annabelle's. "Just wanted to say hey. I'm shutting off the monitor because you should be watching the street anyway."

Clara checked her watch. "There's only nine minutes left until Patient X's appointment. Do you think you can pick the lock?"

"Pick the lock? Sure. I can *pick the lock*. And as soon as it's picked, the alarm will go off and Stan will be up here before you can say 'Handi Wipes.' I have to disable the alarm system first, don't I? Oh, and by the way, I made sure to rap my knuckles against every spare inch of Stan's desk, just for fun. He's probably gone through a whole box of Handi Wipes already, trying to remove my filthy germs!"

"Just hurry, Annabelle," Clara said, her anxiety returning at the mention of Stan. She suddenly was aware of all her nerve endings, could feel them stretched across her body like a fidgety vine. She kept one eye on the street, watching for cars that might pull up, or a woman who might be headed for 464 Fifth Avenue, while straining to hear Annabelle's progress inside the building. Soft plunking sounds could be heard through the Spyfocals.

"What are you doing, Annabelle?" she whispered.

By way of an answer, the screen on the glasses came on again, and she could see Annabelle holding up a box with a keypad on it. There were wires coming out of the box, and these were attached to another box with a keypad, attached to the wall outside Dr. Piff's office—the alarm box. Annabelle was tapping in some numbers on the keypad—the soft plunking sound—and in a second a message ran across the alarm-box screen: *Password cleared.* Then the screen showed Annabelle's hands holding a metal device, which she stuck in the door's keyhole and flicked a few times. Dr. Piff's door opened. Then the video shut off.

"Show's over for now," Annabelle said. "Keep your eyes peeled."

The next few minutes were excruciating. Every sound that Clara heard through the glasses made her jump. The street was still quiet though—no sign of Patient X yet. Clara checked her watch: 7:56. She should be arriving any minute now. The timing was very, very tight. The masked burglar icon was probably right: their chances for success were lousy. And yet, Clara thought with a quiet thrill, they might just be able to do it. A tiny smile nudged at the corner of her lips. She could understand why Annabelle didn't want to stop being a burglar.

"Oi, you!" a voice said. "Get out of there. Now." A flashlight was shining directly into Clara's face, so that for a second she was blinded. She blinked against the glare, lowering her gaze to avoid it, and saw the perfectly shined black shoes, the navy blue pants, crisply pressed, and clipped to the man's belt hook a gun holster, with the gun quite evidently inside of it.

"I said, now." The voice was calm and menacing. Clara scrambled out of the 6 so fast that her sneakers squeaked loudly against the metal. She could hear Annabelle's voice coming through the Spyfocals' transmitter: "Clara? What's happening out there? Is something wrong?"

The flashlight went off, and Clara, now standing on the sidewalk, slowly raised her eyes. Stan Heckle was even bigger than he looked on-screen, and his pasty-pale skin had a shellacked, shiny look. He reached out and snatched the glasses off Clara's face, then hurled them into the sidewalk gutter, where they landed with a crack and snapped in half.

"Which office is she burgling, then?" he demanded.

"I don't know what you're talking about," Clara said. She was backing away from him slowly, but his hand shot out and grabbed the front of her shirt. He shook her hard, so that the panda bear's black pupils clacked wildly inside their eyeball globes.

"Don't be clever, love, or I'll crack you in two like them bloody Spyfocals," he warned. How did he know they were Spyfocals? Clara wondered.

Then, as if he guessed her thoughts, he smiled, showing teeth that were small and very white and looked as though they had been filed square. "Nice little piece of equipment, them Spyfocals. Cost a pretty penny, too. Now, a smart burglar, which you obviously ain't, should have known that I was once in the thieving racket meself, and that I'd spot a pair of Spyfocals like *that*." He snapped his fingers. His hard gray eyes searched hers for a minute, as if waiting for her to object, and then he added, "Well, perhaps not *just* like that. It took me a moment to suss it out, after I let your partner in crime into the building. But then I said to meself, Stan, where there is one pair of Spyfocals, there must be another, mustn't there? And here you are."

Suddenly, his other hand shot out and fastened to her throat. "I'll ask you once more—what office is she burgling?" His grip tightened, and her breath rattled painfully in her throat.

"My name is Emily McBickle, and I'm lead soprano in the Sandusky—"

His grip around her throat tightened a fraction. "Your windpipe is a millimeter away from being crushed entirely. Do you know how little a millimeter is? Of course not. You Americans have never bothered to learn the metric system, have you? Well, let's just say that a millimeter is a very, very little bit. *Infinitesimally* little."

She was pulling her breath in with a horrible, pathetic sound, like a heavy metal chair scraping against a floor. She felt herself grow light-headed, and it occurred to her that in another moment she would probably pass out. She had only to say three words—*Dr. Piff's office*—and he would release her. Just three short words and she could breathe a whole deep breath. It was so easy. But she simply couldn't do it.

He adjusted his arms, readying himself for the final, fatal squeeze. It was then, when he raised his arm slightly, that Clara spotted a flash of white poking out from the inside pocket of his jacket.

Packets of Handi Wipes.

There were many things that Clara Frankofile, at eleven

years old, had never done before: she had never made a crank phone call, she had never covered her hand with Elmer's glue so that she could peel it off when it dried, and she had never thrown a spitball. But now, approaching the probable end to her improbably short life, Clara collected all the phlegm that she could gather in her mouth, wrapped her tongue around it, and, expelling what little air there was left in her lungs, shot a thick wad of spit directly into Stan Heckle's face. It landed square on his right cheek, frothy and viscous—and full of offensive germs, Clara was sure—and immediately began its sliding descent down his face.

For a moment, Stan was too stunned to do anything. His grip on her throat had not loosened—but it hadn't tightened either. He was struggling over what to do, Clara could see. His jaw tightened, and tiny drops of sweat appeared across his forehead. His eyes dropped to his open jacket, and he looked at the Handi Wipes. He'd need two hands to open the packet and remove the Handi Wipe. Should he release her and wipe away the repulsive wad of seething bacteria? Should he kill her first, and wipe after? Then, to Clara's horror, she felt Stan's grip tighten. He had made his decision: kill her now, wipe later.

But his sudden movement had caused the dripping spit to change its course. It veered to the left as it reached the bottom of his nose and was now heading directly toward Stan's mouth. This was too much for him, and with a wail of disgust, he took his hand from Clara's throat and frantically grabbed for a packet of Handi Wipes.

Clara wasted no time. Inhaling a deep breath, she bolted

toward the office building. She might have run in the other direction. She might have disappeared into the city's dark night, forever out of Stan Heckle's grasp. But Annabelle was inside the building, and Stan knew it, and Clara had to find her before he did.

CHAPTER FOURTEEN

Clara, however, was not quite fast enough. Stan Heckle, having wiped the spit from his face, now stormed through the door of 464 Fifth Avenue and pounced on her, throwing her to the ground and placing his polished black shoes heavily on her back, as though Clara were a prize buck he'd hunted and killed. Or was about to kill.

New York City is an ever-boiling stew of noises: the constant groan of traffic, the impatient pop of taxi horns, the lingering baritone of truck horns, music spilling out of nightclubs, and the hum of a million-odd voices all talking at once. But rarely does one hear the click-clack, click-clacking of a dozen horses galloping at top speed down the middle of Fifth Avenue. Still, there it was. Clara could hear it even with one ear pressed painfully against the lobby floor. In fact, the click-clacking grew so loud that even Stan began to pay attention, and his foot released its pressure just enough so that Clara could lift her head and look out through the glass door to the street.

Outside, just now coming to a halt in front of the doors,

was a band of horses, clad in armor. And riding on their backs were knights—actual knights—also in full metal armor, their helmets and swords glinting under the streetlights.

"It's the bloody Knights of the bloody Round Table, it is!" Stan cried out.

Outside, the knights were dismounting rather awkwardly, the weight of their armor tipping them over, so that several of them crashed to the ground with a tremendous metallic rattle. But the knight who appeared to be the leader—by virtue of the fact that he had the largest helmet and his horse had the most elaborate armor—dismounted with admirable ease and pulled open the front door of 464 Fifth Avenue.

The knight seemed to stare for a moment at Stan and Clara—it was hard to tell, really, because the eye-slit in his visor was very narrow. Then he raised his spear and touched the point of it to Stan's throat.

"Ref yawfa," the knight said.

"Pardon?" Stan replied.

"Ref yawfa mefnie bo," the knight repeated more loudly.

"Sorry, mate, but I can't understand a word you're saying with that helmet on your head."

With his free hand the knight tried to lift the visor in his helmet. It yawned open for a second, then slammed shut again. He tried again while the other knights began to clank in through the front doors, and this time the visor held.

"Remove your foot from Miss Frankofile's back," the knight repeated.

"Prim!" Clara cried. And indeed, peering out from beneath the helmet was the terribly thin and terribly wealthy face of Prim LeDander. Behind her, the other knights lifted their visors as well, and in a minute a dozen of New York's high society ladies—all without eyebrows—were staring at Stan and Clara.

"I said remove your foot, sir," Prim repeated more forcefully, the tip of her spear pointing steadily at Stan's Adam's apple. Stan removed his shoe from Clara's back, and Clara scrambled to her feet and ran over to the knights.

"It is not a bad shoe, actually," said Bitsey Fopah. "The stitching looks well done."

"Ask him where he purchased them," one of the other ladies said.

"Where did you purchase your shoes?" Prim demanded, her spear still touching Stan's throat.

"Ehm, eh . . . London," Stan stammered.

"London!"

"The imported shoes are always the best . . ."

The door opened again, and in rushed reporters with television cameras and microphones, all pushing at each other to get through the door first.

"Is she here?" one television reporter asked breathlessly.

"Is who here?" Clara asked.

"The Face of the Middle Ages. We received a phone call saying that she would be announced now, in this lobby."

"Ha!" cried Prim. "I told you, girls!" Then to Clara, she explained, "I have a friend who writes for the *Times*. He tipped me off about the announcement just after we finished our jousting match in the park. We figured that since one of us is bound to be chosen, it would be a good photo op to arrive on horseback. Very splashy and all. I won the match, incidentally, didn't I, ladies?" Her jousting spear was still touching Stan's throat, and this bit of news did not make him any happier.

"Look! That must be her!" one of the cameramen shouted, and he pointed to a long black limousine pulling up just outside the building. The door opened, and a woman wearing a black shawl over her head and a black dress stepped out. The cameramen and reporters rushed out, shining their bright lights on the woman.

"Isn't that June Loblolly?" Bitsey asked.

"Yes, it is," Clara confirmed.

Outside, poor June Loblolly was staring in horror at the scads of cameramen and reporters running up to her. After all, she had meant to arrive in secrecy for her appointment with Dr. Muster to have her nose bobbed, her lips poufed, and her cheekbones cheekier, to make her not-quite-beautiful face appear less sad to the American public.

CHAPTER FIFTEEN

Amidst the sudden rush of reporters and cameramen, Clara felt a hand grip her elbow, and a voice in her ear cried, "Run!"

Clara turned around quickly, and there was Annabelle. She had never been so happy to see someone in her life.

"Come on!" Annabelle urged, pulling at her elbow. "Run!"

They broke through the crowd and flew down the street. Behind them they could hear Stan yelling, "Oi! Them two is thieves!" (But clever Prim had not removed her jousting sword from his throat, in part because it gave her something to do while she hid her tears from the cameras outside—she had been *so* sure that she was going to be chosen as the Face of the Middle Ages.)

Clara and Annabelle ran across the street and dashed into the subway station, running so fast down the stairs that Annabelle tripped and landed on her backside at the landing. But she picked herself up nimbly and they swiped their card in the turnstile. Luck appeared to be on their side, because a train was just pulling into the station.

They collapsed in a double seat in the corner, breathing so heavily that neither one could speak. Looking at each other, they smiled, and then laughed so hard that the young couple sitting across from them broke the subway rule and stared at them.

It was a strange, exhilarating feeling to have come so close to danger and yet have escaped unharmed. Clara felt her blood moving faster through her body, her brain standing at attention.

"Wow, that was something, huh? All those knights coming just at that moment!" Clara exclaimed. "You wouldn't believe it, but Stan Heckle almost killed me. Honestly, I was this close to winding up in the Hudson River! And then, out of nowhere, I heard the horses . . . and then Prim and . . . oh, that was about the luckiest thing I've ever heard of!"

"Luck?" Annabelle blurted out. "Cripes, you are thick!"

"What do you mean?"

"All those reporters didn't just happen to arrive by luck. *I* called them when I heard Stan's voice through your Spyfocals. I gave them an anonymous tip that the Face of the Middle Ages was going to be announced in the lobby of 464 Fifth Avenue, pronto. In my opinion, it's best to have a crowd around when you're dealing with someone who might separate your head from your body. All those women arriving on horseback—now, *that* was just pure, dumb luck."

"But how did you know about the Face of the Middle Ages?"

"Like I tried to tell you earlier, I did my research, thank you very much. You know, burgling isn't just about breaking and entering. It's about escaping, too. Anyway," Annabelle admitted, "when Dad and I went to that party in your building, it was the only thing those loopy old, rich broads were talking about. Half of them had even shaved their eyebrows off!"

"They waxed them," Clara corrected.

"Did they? Jeez, that's even worse."

In all the ruckus, Clara had forgotten about the envelope. Now she turned to Annabelle eagerly and asked, "So? Did you get it?"

Annabelle patted her bag. "Easy peasy."

"I spit at Stan," Clara said after a minute. "I've never spit at someone before."

"You need to get out more."

Back at Annabelle's house, they sneaked in quietly and crept upstairs. In her bedroom, Annabelle kicked off her heels, and Clara—regretfully—took off her sneakers, and the two of them collapsed onto the bed. Annabelle squeezed her arm down the narrow space between her bed and the wall, and when her hand came up again, it was gripping a box with a picture of a rectangular brown food on it.

"Pop-Tarts?" Clara read the box. She made a face. "It's not good for your immune system, is it?"

"It *fries* your immune system! Don't tell me you've never eaten a Pop-Tart before."

"I don't eat things that come out of boxes."

"Kid"—Annabelle opened the box and pulled out a foil-wrapped rectangle. She ripped the wrapper with her teeth, pulled out a Pop-Tart, and handed it to Clara—"welcome to the world."

The world, as it turned out, tasted pretty great. Annabelle reached down behind her bed again and pulled out a cello-phane pack of red sticks, which she said were Twizzlers; a somewhat smooshed package of tiny chocolate-glazed dough-nuts; and a bag of pork rinds.

"Hey, a girl can't live on spirulina alone," Annabelle explained, spreading the feast out on the bed. Then she reached into her tote bag on the floor and pulled out the thick manila envelope.

"And I didn't peek in it, in case you're wondering," Annabelle said. She handed the envelope to Clara, then picked up a teen magazine off the floor and buried her nose in it.

Clara took a deep breath, then uncoiled the string from the round clasp.

There were many papers inside, almost all of them dated, and apparently in chronological order. Clara thought it best to start at the beginning. She pulled out the first page, which was closest to the front of the envelope and had the earliest date marked on top of it, and began to read the neatly printed handwriting:

June 8, 1985
    The elderly Ms. Emma Fizzelli asked me to examine her cook, Audrey Aster, whose eyesight had been

deteriorating. The young woman came to my office today. Ran tests, but see nothing obviously wrong.

Fizzelli? Why was that name so familiar, Clara wondered. Then she realized it was the same last name of the artist who had once lived in Pish Posh's building.

Below that, and on several pages after, were columns of numbers and technical names that Clara did not understand. Probably test results of some kind.

Then, scribbled hastily on the back of one of the pages:

June 11, 1985

Appointment with Audrey Aster to discuss results of her tests. Am prescribing stronger lenses for her glasses. Otherwise, eyes are healthy.

When patient is given the results, she becomes very upset. Close to tears. Ms. Aster says it's not just her eyesight that is poor. Her other senses have been weakening, too. She can hardly taste her food anymore—as if tongue has gone numb. Sense of smell is growing weaker, and her ears feel as though they are filled with water. Says she forgot to put mitts on before pulling a pan of muffins out of the oven the other day, and felt nothing more than a small tingle. I am horrified to see that there is indeed a searing red mark across the palm of her hand and ugly blisters on her fingertips.

"It is like I am fading away, a little at a time," Ms. Aster says.

I suggest she see a neurologist, but the young woman refuses. Says that Ms. Fizzelli told her I am the only doctor she can trust, the only one who will understand her predicament.

"What predicament is that?" I ask. But the young woman becomes hysterical, sobbing, and I can get no more out of her. I'm afraid she may be emotionally unstable—perhaps dangerously so.

The following page read:

June 12, 1985
Spoke to Emma Fizzelli about her cook. Tried to get more information about the young woman's state of mind. The conversation, however, took a strange turn. Here it is, to the word, as best as I can recall:
"How well do you know Ms. Aster?" I asked.
"I've known dear Audrey since I was a tiny baby."
"You mean you've known her since *she* was a tiny baby," I corrected.
"I meant what I said the first time," Ms. Fizzelli insisted.
"But how can that be?" I asked as gently as I could. "Your cook is twenty-four years old, and you are seventy-seven."
"Well, I know how old I am, Doctor." She laughed at me. "I've been there for all my seventy-seven birthdays, and Audrey has baked me a lemon cake with

white frosting for each and every one. She did the same for my mother and my grandmother and my great-grandmother as well. The fact is she has been with our family for generations, Doctor. I believe we have kept her secret admirably, and I ask that you do the same."

"But what you are telling me is impossible," I countered.

"The world is full of impossible things, my dear Dr. Piff. Do what you can for her. I expect no more."

I'm afraid Ms. Fizzelli's mind is not what it used to be. However, I told her I will do my best, but that may not be very much.

Clara had been reading so raptly that she had forgotten about her Pop-Tart. She popped the rest of it into her mouth, then pulled a Twizzler out of its package.

"Anything good in there?" Annabelle asked, lifting her head from the magazine.

Clara nodded and, after biting into the Twizzler, which was a little like biting into a strawberry-flavored electrical cord, continued reading. There were many more entries documenting Audrey's other visits to Dr. Piff's office. It seemed, however, that nothing too dramatic happened until November 17, 1990:

Ms. Fizzelli passed away this morning at the ripe old age of eighty-two. A sad passing for all, but saddest for Audrey Aster. The Fizzelli mansion is to be sold to a restaurateur named Pierre Frankofile, I am told, and the upstairs made into apartments. Ms. Aster is terrified of having to leave. She says that sitting by her window and watching the park is the only thing that gives her any pleasure. I don't know why, but there is something about the young woman that makes me feel protective of her. Perhaps I can work something out with Mr. Frankofile.

Work something out with her father? What would he work out? Clara turned the page, and her question was answered immediately.

> February 3, 1991
> Well, I have done it. After much haggling and unpleasantness (indeed, Mr. Frankofile is a difficult man, to say the least), I have struck a deal with him. He will allow Audrey to continue to live in the mansion, in a small apartment above the restaurant, if she will work for him in his restaurant for very little pay. The rumor is that he has a hard time keeping employees, because he is so difficult. Audrey has agreed, and I do believe all will be well.
> Her condition seems to have stabilized. I am beginning to grow more hopeful.

After that there were pages and pages of things that Clara could not make heads or tails of, mostly medications and tests, she guessed. Here and there a few brief notes:

Complains of numbness in her hands again. Vision fuzzy.

Then . . .

November 9, 2000
I have now known Audrey Aster for fifteen years, and I can no longer deny it. Though her condition worsens, she has not aged at all since I first met her. How is this possible? I am beginning to wonder if Ms. Fizzelli's odd story is true.

January 7, 2002
I have tried everything—pills, tonics, even herbs from China—but Audrey does not respond. Her condition grows increasingly worse. Her sense of smell and taste are gone completely, and her eyesight is weakening rapidly. I do believe she will go completely blind within a few years. What will happen to her then? Frankofile will certainly fire her from Pish Posh. That would be the worst possible thing I can imagine! She'll be forced to leave the house, and that will surely destroy her.

I only wish that the Frankofiles' daughter were older. She's a sweet-tempered child of great compassion (which she certainly did not inherit from her parents), and she might have been a great help to Audrey—someone who would have kept her secret safe and seen to it that she remained in the house.

The last passage took Clara by surprise. How odd it was to hear someone describe her that way. She smiled a little, then quickly glanced over at Annabelle, embarrassed. But Annabelle was too engrossed in her magazine to notice.

Next came notes from a medical conference, and several more tests. Then, on March 18th, 2005:

Another sad note: Clara Frankofile is a dismal disappointment. This child who once showed such promise has grown into a hard and unforgiving girl, trumped up like a tiny thirty-year-old snob. I pity her.

Clara's face burned bright red. A mixture of rage and embarrassment flooded her body. How *dare* he pity her?!

She gathered up the papers and shoved them back in the envelope.

"What's wrong?" Annabelle asked.

"Nothing." Clara turned away so Annabelle wouldn't see how red her face had become. "I'm tired. Can we shut off the light?"

"Sure," Annabelle said. She closed the magazine and shut off the light, and the two of them climbed under the covers.

Much as she tried, though, Clara could not get Dr. Piff's words out of her head. She felt an odd crumply feeling around her throat and a wettish tickle creep across her cheek-bone. She swiped her hand across it quickly, but it came again, faster and faster, and she could not stop it. I'm crying, she thought, stunned. Stop it, she told herself. You are not an infant. You *will* stop crying, you *must* stop crying! But though the tears were part of her body, they seemed to govern themselves. Utterly humiliated, there was nothing left for Clara to do but turn away from Annabelle and let the tears flow—which they did, long after Annabelle was snoring.

CHAPTER SIXTEEN

The next morning, Clara sat down to breakfast in the kitchen. Mr. Arbutnot had made twelve-grain hot cereal, which tasted like a cross between wet bread and beach sand. It was topped with soy nuts and chased with a tall glass of watery-looking rice milk.

"You're not eating your breakfast." Mr. Arbutnot nodded toward Clara's barely touched bowl of cereal.

"I'm not very hungry," she muttered. Which was actually true. Her stomach felt knotted up, and her eyelids were swollen and hot-feeling from crying.

"Soy nuts are good for lots of medical ailments," Mr. Arbutnot said. "Like fungus, for instance."

Clara turned to Annabelle angrily, but Annabelle deliberately avoided her eyes and gazed down at the newspaper on the table instead.

"Hey, look at that!" she said and read the headline: "Metropolitan Museum of Art Announces Its Face of the Middle Ages." She held the paper up for them to see. There was a picture of June Loblolly, looking stunned as she stood outside the 464 Fifth Avenue office. Although she hadn't been *officially* selected, all the hoopla must have convinced the Met that they had found their woman.

Mr. Arbutnot considered the picture for a moment, then said, "Well, I guess she does have a certain look about her. But if the Met wanted to find a *real* Face of the Middle Ages, they'd have been better off finding someone with missing teeth and greasy hair. I have a patient who was a nursemaid in 1402, and she said she bathed once a year and cleaned her teeth with the end of a twig."

After breakfast Clara asked to use the phone, first spending a few moments perusing the Manhattan phone book. Blurt, it turned out, was a most uncommon name. In fact, there was only one Blurt listed: Shelly Blurt. Clara dialed the number. The phone rang so many times that Clara nearly hung up, but finally there was a breathless voice on the other end.

"Yes?"

"Ms. Blurt?" Clara asked.

"Yes?"

"This is Clara Frankofile. I need to talk to you."

Ms. Blurt hesitated. "Oh? What about?" It sounded like she was trying very hard to sound nonchalant.

"The other night, when you fainted—"

"It was all the excitement, I'm sure," Ms. Blurt cut in nervously.

"It was the soup cook, Ms. Blurt, let's not pretend. You must tell me what you know about her." Clara thought it best to be stern with Ms. Blurt.

"If I did . . . no, really, the whole thing is impossible," said Ms. Blurt.

"Ms. Blurt, the world is full of impossible things." Clara repeated Ms. Fizzelli's words with a conviction that surprised even herself. There was a pause on the other end.

"All right. But I'll have to show you, rather than tell you. Can you come to my apartment?"

Ms. Blurt gave Clara her address. It wasn't far from Annabelle's.

"I'll be there in ten minutes," Clara said.

Ms. Blurt lived in a tiny one-room apartment, up five steep flights of stairs. The stairway smelled of tuna casserole and cat litter, and all the doors had at least half-a-dozen locks on them.

By the time she reached Ms. Blurt's apartment, Clara was fairly out of breath from the climb and queasy from the odor. She knocked on the door, panting a little, and listened as the locks in Ms. Blurt's apartment clicked and snapped for a full minute before the door opened.

Ms. Blurt was wearing a pink pantsuit with a giant green butterfly sewn on to the bottoms of her pants' legs and a matching butterfly on the pocket of her jacket. Multicolored butterfly barrettes were sprinkled through her mass of wild hair, their silver antennas wiggling.

"Come in, come in," she said hastily, and she hustled Clara inside the apartment. "I'm still looking for it . . . I know it's around here somewhere . . . Sit down, sit down . . ." Ms. Blurt indicated a small brown sofa in the middle of the room that was completely surrounded by thick mounds of books, magazines, and papers, strewn all across the floor. "Just be careful not to step on anything," she added.

Not to step on anything? There didn't seem to be any bare floor to put your foot upon. Still, Ms. Blurt trotted off easily through the clutter and began to scour a bookcase that covered the entire back wall.

Clara looked down and saw that indeed there were bits of green carpet peeking through the clutter, and that the bits of green formed a trail, rather like stepping-stones across a stream, that led directly to the couch. Another trail, the one that Ms. Blurt had taken, wound its way around to the bookshelf with smaller branches that led to the tiny kitchen and an even tinier bathroom.

Clara took the trail to the couch, staring down at the reading material as she planted her feet on one spot of green carpet after the next. The books and magazines were all about art—Renaissance art, primitive art, impressionist art. What was odd was that Ms. Blurt had no artwork at all on the walls. Instead, the walls were covered with different colored Post-it notes, scrawled with cryptic messages: *Was the musician in Giancarlo's painting a local pickpocket in Venice?* and *The princess with the golden hair in DePonsy's portrait looks bored, but really she was very ill and probably feverish. She died right after the portrait was painted.*

Clara sat down on the couch and waited, watching Ms. Blurt frantically pawing through the bookshelf. The books were lying every which way, crammed across horizontally and stacked vertically, with still other books balanced precariously on the scant space along the edge of the shelf.

"Here it is!" Ms. Blurt exclaimed, pulling out a fat, hardbound book that had many pages marked off with paper clips. She tucked the book beneath her arm and stepped nimbly through the clutter to sit beside Clara on the couch.

Clara caught the title of the book before Ms. Blurt opened it: *The Complete Collection of American Nineteenth Century Paintings*. After a few moments of leafing through the pages, Ms. Blurt stopped at a glossy reproduction of a painting. She smoothed out the page and carefully placed the book on Clara's lap.

Clara looked at the painting but failed to see anything extraordinary. The caption below the painting read "*St. Theresa and the Angel*, painted 1817," and it showed an angel holding an arrow and bending over a swooning barefoot young woman dressed in a white robe.

Clara shrugged. "So?"

"Look at St. Theresa carefully. The one who's fainting," Ms. Blurt urged.

Clara looked at her face. Then she frowned and dipped her head to look more closely.

"Oh!" she exclaimed.

"Do you see it?" Ms. Blurt asked excitedly.

Well, really, how could you not? Clara thought. Yet it was impossible!

"Obviously, I could find no explanation for it," Ms. Blurt

said, "and I thought it best not to say anything until I could. But now that you've seen it, too, I admit I'm relieved. I was beginning to wonder if I'd been wrong . . ."

No, Ms. Blurt had not been wrong, Clara thought. St. Theresa looked *exactly* like Audrey Aster, right down to that odd check mark–shaped scar on her chin.

"And there are other paintings of her, too." Ms. Blurt grabbed the book and flipped through it, showing Clara at least a dozen other paintings that featured the same model. In one she was posed as a peasant woman buying vegetables in a market, in another she was Eve sitting on a stone wall in the Garden of Eden, staring up at an apple dangling from a tree. And in yet another she was Juliet from *Romeo and Juliet*, standing on a terrace entwined with flowering vines, clad in a nightgown, her arms stretched up to the stars. There were different poses, different costumes, yet in each and every painting the woman was the spitting image of Audrey.

"But this makes no sense," Clara said.

"None whatsoever!" agreed Ms. Blurt. Her voice sounded almost hysterical. "So I began to do a little research. Researching the people who modeled for painters is a little hobby of mine." She flourished a hand around at the Post-it–covered walls, and the books and magazines on the floor. "Of course, it makes life a little messy at times."

"A little," Clara agreed.

"In any case, it was hard to find anything on Caleb Fizzelli's model. He isn't exactly well known, though if there were any justice in the world, he would be." Ms. Blurt closed her eyes and shook her head. "Such a gifted man!

There's a portrait of him somewhere, in one of these magazines . . ."

She gazed around at the floor, and seemed in imminent danger of beginning another search until Clara reminded her: "The woman in the paintings, Ms. Blurt. Did you find out something about her?"

"Oh, yes, and it's a strange story, too. I discovered it in a letter that Fizzelli wrote to a friend. It seems that when he moved into his house in New York at the end of September, in 1812, he found a woman sitting by herself in one of the rooms. He asked her who she was and she said she didn't know, that she had simply awakened one day in a bedroom upstairs. The house was entirely empty and quiet, but the pantry was stocked—and she wondered by whom, since not another soul was around. She told Fizzelli that she had been living like this for days, all alone, wandering through the rooms, staring out the window and hoping for a clue to appear that would tell her who she was.

"He explained to her that he'd purchased the house and was to move in the following week, but the woman flatly refused to leave. I guess he took pity on her, and he decided to keep her on as a boarder. Instead of paying rent, he said she could pose for him, because he liked her face, despite the fact that she had a prominent scar on her chin." Ms. Blurt took a long deep breath and stopped.

"And was that all he said about her?" Clara asked.

Ms. Blurt nodded, and the butterfly antennas in her hair wobbled crazily.

"Ms. Blurt," Clara said, "I need to borrow this book."

Clara reached out, took the book from Ms. Blurt's lap before she could say no, and started down the trail of green carpet toward the door.

"Oh, but you will be careful with it, won't you?" Ms. Blurt called nervously after her. "Don't remove any of the paper clips, and there are several Post-it notes on the pages, and the most important thing to remember is . . ."

But Clara was out the door before she could find out what that might be.

CHAPTER SEVENTEEN

"Annabelle, tell me the truth. Can your father really hypnotize people?" Clara had called Annabelle's house as soon as she got home.

"He's a better thief than a hypnotist," Annabelle said in such a strident voice that Clara knew her dad must be standing right there.

"Can I speak to him?" Clara said. Getting a straight answer from Annabelle on this matter was going to be difficult.

"What do you want to speak to him about?" Annabelle asked suspiciously.

"Just about . . . a woman," Clara said evasively.

"What woman?" Annabelle asked sharply. "Is she rich? Do you want him to steal something from her?"

"Annabelle, can you just put him on?"

Thankfully, Mr. Arbutnot took the phone out of his daughter's hand and asked Clara what he could do for her.

"I can't hypnotize *all* people," Mr. Arbutnot replied to her question. "They have to be willing, of course. And some people just seem to resist it naturally. But yes, I can hypnotize *most* people."

In the background, Clara heard Annabelle wail, "Don't encourage him, for cripes' sake!"

"Would you be able to hypnotize someone who doesn't remember who she is?" Clara asked.

"Someone with amnesia, you mean?" Mr. Arbutnot sounded intrigued. "Hmmm. I've never worked with an amnesia case before. I'd be willing to give it a whirl."

"Do you think you can hypnotize her in her home?" Clara asked. "Today, maybe?"

"As a matter of fact, my afternoon's clear. Where does she live?"

Clara gave him Pish Posh's address, which he repeated. In the background she heard Annabelle yell, "I hate you, Clara!"

"She doesn't really," Mr. Arbutnot said.

"I know," Clara replied.

It was early afternoon and Pish Posh was empty—no staff, no customers. The tables were all covered with crisp white linen and set with gleaming silverware. Everything was still and quiet.

"So this is the famous Pish Posh restaurant?" Mr. Arbutnot said, looking around. He seemed a little disappointed. "It's not quite what I expected."

"It looks different when the people get here," Clara explained. Even to her eyes, though, she could see that the restaurant lacked its usual dazzle. She hated to admit it, but without the customers, the restaurant looked pretty ordinary, just like any other nice restaurant in New York City.

Clara led Mr. Arbutnot up the kitchen stairs and pounded hard on Audrey's door with the side of her fist.

"Take it easy there, sport," Mr. Arbutnot said, looking at her askance.

"She won't hear otherwise."

The door opened and Audrey appeared with a sketchbook under her arm and clutching a stick of charcoal. She gazed at Clara, squinting a little through her glasses, then confusedly over at Mr. Arbutnot.

"If you're here to fire me again—" Audrey began.

"This is Dr. Arbutnot," Clara hastened to reply. Well, it wasn't quite true that he was a doctor, but close enough, Clara reasoned. "I brought him here because I think he might be able to help you."

"Help me with what?" Audrey frowned, squinting from one to the other. "Anyway, I have a doctor."

Dr. Piff. Of course, Clara realized, Audrey didn't know. Clara lifted her glasses and propped them up on her head. It was the sort of news that you couldn't give behind a pair of large dark sunglasses.

"Dr. Piff died, Audrey," Clara said. "A few days ago. He had a heart attack."

Audrey's lower lip dropped a little. She turned and sat down in her rocking chair by the window. In silence she dropped her sketch pad and charcoal on the floor beside her—a quick, sad gesture. A gesture of defeat.

Clara looked down at the sketch pad. All you could really

make out were vague blobby figures and a long tubular shape, which Clara guessed was the old elm tree. For a while the only sound in the room was the uneven bumping of the rocking chair as Audrey rocked, staring blindly out the window.

"Did Dr. Piff tell you about me, then?" Audrey asked finally. There was a note of resentment in her voice.

"Dr. Piff never told me anything about you," Clara said, which was true, after all. "But there's this." Clara opened Ms. Blurt's book to the painting of St. Theresa and put it on Audrey's lap. Audrey looked down at it, and then brought the book close to her face to see.

"Oh!" she exhaled softly. "I haven't seen this in so long . . ." As she turned the pages, her face flushed and a smile touched her lips, stretching the scar on her chin upward a bit. It transformed her momentarily. She looked beautiful and unearthly, like a goddess who, much to her amusement, had been plunked down in a musty little room without knowing why. Clara could suddenly see why Caleb Fizzelli had been so quick to strike his deal with her all those years ago. Mr. Arbutnot, too, seemed struck by the woman in front of him. He stared at her, blinking quickly, as if the sun, which was now slowly creeping by the window, were toying with his vision.

Finally, Audrey closed the book and looked up at them. Her smile had vanished.

"I'm tired," she confessed.

"We should leave you then," said Mr. Arbutnot.

"No, that's not what I mean. I mean . . . I'm tired of life. I know you can't imagine such a thing. My body is young, but my soul is old." Her eyes flitted around the room, as if she were seeking something that her dimming vision could not find. "I suppose there must have been a time when things were different. When I took pleasure in the feel of the sun on my skin or the crunch of snow under my boots. When I laughed easily at silly things. But if I ever felt like that, I can't remember, so what good is it to me?"

Clara understood. She understood so well, in fact, that for the first time in her life—or at least the first time she could remember—her heart actually ached for another person. She looked over at Mr. Arbutnot anxiously.

"What do you think?" she asked him. "Can you help her?"

"The sooner we get started," he said, pulling up an armchair near Audrey's rocker, "the sooner we'll find out."

"Ready?" Mr. Arbutnot asked.

"Do I have to close my eyes?" Audrey asked uneasily.

"Only if you want to."

She did, and then Mr. Arbutnot began.

"Imagine that you are floating on your back in the middle of a lake, on a warm sunny day . . . ," he started. His voice was calm, soft. "Your body begins to sink beneath the water, slowly, peacefully. You have no trouble breathing. As you sink deeper and deeper, you are moving backward in time: yesterday, the week before, the year before, way back, year by year . . ." He went on like this for some time until Audrey's eyes opened abruptly.

"We've hit some turbulence," Mr. Arbutnot said quietly to Clara.

137

"Is that bad?" she asked.

He shook his head. "On the contrary." Then he said, "Tell me what you see, Audrey."

"Don't call me Audrey," Audrey said, with some annoyance.

"Isn't that your name?"

"No. I gave myself that name later, much later . . ."

"What's your real name, then?" Mr. Arbutnot asked.

"Theodosia. Theodosia Pender. You may call me Miss Pender."

"Miss Pender, where are you?"

"Right here, of course."

"I mean, where do you live?"

"Right *here*," she said impatiently. "In this house. Where else would I be?"

"My apologies. What are you doing this evening?"

"I'm to have a party."

"And what will you wear?"

Audrey smiled. "The loveliest blue velvet gown trimmed with satin of a deeper blue. It was made in Paris. What do you think? Isn't it charming?" She had not moved a muscle, but there was great animation in her face.

"It looks terrific on you," Mr. Arbutnot said.

"I know it does. Do you think I'm conceited?" she asked archly.

"No, just honest," Mr. Arbutnot replied.

"Exactly! Most people are horrible liars. Look how well the dress goes with my necklace. It makes the diamonds shine beautifully." She touched her neck, which was bare. "My mother gave this necklace to me before she died. My father is dead, too, as I'm sure you know."

"No, I didn't know. Please tell me about your party, Miss Pender."

"Dull, dull, dull! But I find most people stupid in general."

Clara blushed. Miss Pender sounded a little bit like Clara herself. She wondered for a moment if Audrey was making fun of her.

"Is she really under hypnosis?" Clara asked Mr. Arbutnot. He nodded and put his finger to his lips.

"We are all in the parlor," Audrey continued. "Some people are playing cards while one man is playing the piano and singing a ballad. Everyone is talking about the same dreary things: about the shameful way that pigs are allowed to roam the streets of New York City. About the woman who was murdered in her room on Clarkson Street, and how Regency hats with their ostrich feather are all the rage, and blah, blah, blah."

For a moment Mr. Arbutnot seemed confused.

"Miss Pender, what is the date?" he asked.

"The sixth of September."

"And the year, Miss Pender?"

"1812."

Mr. Arbutnot smiled. "Ah."

"Someone new has just come in with my cousin. A young man. My cousin introduces him to me as Frank Ploy. He is tall and slim and dressed in an elegant yellow waistcoat, knee breeches, long boots, and a white ruffled shirt. His face is handsome. But somehow . . . rough.

"'Miss Pender,' he says when he greets me, 'your cousin has told me so much about you that I insisted upon meeting you.'

"'Oh?' I glance wryly at my cousin, who has now turned very red. 'Did my cousin tell you that I am rude and intolerant, and that though I am terribly wealthy, I have managed to frighten away every young man in New York City through my bad temper? Is that what he told you?'

"I expect Frank Ploy to hem and haw, but he looks at me straight in the eye and says, 'Yes. And much worse, too.' Then he smiles, and I like him instantly. What do you think of him?"

"A very likable fellow," Mr. Arbutnot agreed.

"Yes, exactly. Very likable. My cousin leaves us to mingle with the other guests. Frank Ploy looks at me and smiles.

"'Already I can see that we have much in common,' he says cheerfully.

"'What do you mean?' I ask.

"'We are both scarred,' he says, indicating the scar on my chin—an old injury from a boy who threw a rock at me when I was a child.

"'But I see no scars on you,' I reply.

"Then he extends his right hand toward me and makes a fist. His knuckles are covered with small silvery scars, as though a crazed seamstress had sewn it willy-nilly with fine silver thread.

"He tells me, in a quiet voice, that he was born under the

very poorest conditions, and as a young boy became a bare-knuckle boxer on the streets of New York. He was very good, I suppose, because he managed to make money. Quite a bit of money. He fought in England and France and eventually grew rather wealthy.

"'I can never forget who I was,' he says, 'because it is etched across my fist.'

"At first I am alarmed to hear this. That means he is not one of *us*, regardless of his beautiful clothing and fine manners. Yet, as we speak further, I begin to think that although he isn't my equal, he may perhaps be *better* than my friends and me, because we have done nothing to earn our wealth, and he has struggled so hard for his.

"Every now and then we are interrupted by someone who wishes to chat with me. It's annoying, as I have no interest in them, and to escape from their attentions, I ask Mr. Ploy if he would like to see the garden while there is still some light outside.

"He readily agrees, and I take him to our little courtyard. We walk around the garden while we talk and talk, and finally sit beside each other on a bench, surrounded by beautiful asters, which have only lately begun to bloom—starry lavender, blue, and pink.

"'They were my mother's favorite flower,' I tell him. 'She planted masses of them while she was ill. To remind me of her each year. She gave me this necklace, too, right before she died. She wanted me to wait till I was married to wear it, but because I am the most sharp-tongued, cold-hearted woman in all of New York, I decided it would be silly to wait.'

"'Funny,' Mr. Ploy says, touching my necklace briefly and looking at me with great seriousness, 'I am tremendously fond of ladies with sharp tongues and cold hearts.'

"We talk until it grows so dark that even the bright asters fade into the shadows. When we return to the house, I find my guests have all gone. Oh, I'm certain my disappearance will be the talk of the town for weeks to come, but I don't care!

"When we part, Mr. Ploy wonders if he might visit me again the next day. I should refuse, shouldn't I?"

"Well, that depends upon how you feel about him, Miss Pender," Mr. Arbutnot replied.

"You may call me Theodosia now that we know each other better."

"Thank you," Mr. Arbutnot said graciously. "How do you feel about him, Theodosia?"

"I like him," Audrey said firmly, her face glowing. "I allow I have never liked a person so much in my life! I agree to see him again tomorrow. Are you terribly shocked?"

"Not in the least."

"After he leaves, I rush up to my bedroom and lean out the window to watch him as he walks down the street. In the yellowish glow of the streetlamps, I can see him walking slowly yet with purpose, holding himself straight—not like so many of the men I know who pretend to be rakes, and slouch and swagger.

"It is when I ready myself for bed that evening that I discover my necklace is missing. I look everywhere for it, then wake the servants and entreat them to search as well. It is nowhere to be found. How perplexing! I think back to when

I last knew the necklace was around my throat. Then I remember—it was when Frank Ploy touched it, in the garden. Oh." She placed a hand against her stomach and winced. "I feel sick suddenly.

"I can't sleep that night, I am so consumed with the problem. As the hours pass, I grow more and more convinced that I have been the victim of a swindler. I've heard about such men before. When he touched my necklace in the garden, he might have cunningly cut it with palm clippers, a thing I have read about in the newspapers. By the morning, I can no longer lie to myself. I *know* that Frank Ploy is a thief. He flirted with me and flattered me so that he might steal from me! He made a fool of me. I cannot tolerate that! You understand, don't you?"

"Of course," Mr. Arbutnot said.

"As soon as I am dressed, I go directly to the constables and tell them what has happened.

"A few days later, on my way to the milliner to have a hat made, I glance at the front of a newsboy's *Evening Post* and see Frank Ploy's face on the front of it. The headline reads, 'Man Arrested for Stealing Jewels from New York's Most Prominent Young Heiress.' The article says that he is also suspected of murdering the woman on Clarkson Street, because he lived in a boardinghouse nearby and jewels were also stolen from her room.

"I am shocked. He was in my house. Alone with me. He might have murdered me as well."

"You were lucky, Theodosia," Mr. Arbutnot said solemnly.

"I know." Audrey stopped here, and it seemed as if she were finished. But then her hand rose up to her chest and her breathing quickened.

"Is she okay?" Clara whispered to Mr. Arbutnot. He nodded shortly.

"What is happening now, Theodosia?" Mr. Arbutnot asked.

"Today is the day that they are to execute Frank Ploy. He will be hanged from a tree in Washington Square Park at noon. Not for murder—they failed to convict him on that charge. But the punishment for theft is harsh. And rightly so! The city would be full of savages otherwise.

"I am keeping myself busy around the house, checking to see that my silverware is polished, that my pantry is full, that my porcelain is dusted. Anything to take my mind off what is to come. But as it grows closer to noon, I can hear the crowds gathering in the park.

"From my bedroom window, I have a clear view of Washington Square Park, as well as the elm tree from which they hang criminals. They call it the Hanging Tree. Oh, there are so many hangings from that elm! Men, women. They always hang them from the same branch, that very thick one there."

Clara took a quick glance out the window. Indeed, there was the tremendous elm tree—the one that Clara had always been mesmerized by—with a branch that was thicker than the others, jutting out like a stern hand, saluting the city. Beneath the tree was the little artist who had offered to draw Clara's portrait, working away on a sketch of a woman who was sitting in a folding chair by his easel.

"I open the window and lean out. A crowd of people is milling around, waiting for the hanging to start, as if it were a show. There is even a woman selling oysters to the spectators. I can see Frank Ploy now. He is being marched from Newgate Prison on Tenth Street to the park. His hands are tied behind his back, but I notice that he still holds himself as upright as possible. I feel a pang as I catch a glimpse of his face, pale but firm. I remind myself that he deserves his punishment, no matter how severe.

"They haul him up a set of stairs to a wooden platform. Above, a rope is lashed to the tree limb, with a noose dangling down. Parents are lifting up their little children to get a better view—how can you bring a child to such a thing? A few words are said to Mr. Ploy—I can't hear them from here—and the hangman puts Mr. Ploy's head into the noose. I can't watch, it's too horrible. I look away, dropping my eyes so that they look down at the street below my window.

"*What is that?*" Audrey cried suddenly, her eyes wide. "Down there. What is that?!"

"What do you see?" Mr. Arbutnot asked.

"Oh, no! Oh, no!" She was breathing hard now and shaking her head.

"Theodosia," he said. "Theodosia! What do you see?"

But Audrey did not seem to hear him anymore. A sheen of sweat had broken out across her face, and she was making a small, whimpering noise.

"What's happening to her?" Clara asked Mr. Arbutnot, trying to keep the panic out of her voice.

"I don't know." To Clara's dismay, he also looked

alarmed, and with a sickish feeling in her stomach, she began to wonder if she had made an awful mistake in bringing him here. Impulsively, she picked up Audrey's sketchbook off the floor and placed it in her lap. Then she grabbed the bit of charcoal and wrapped Audrey's fingers around it.

"Draw it," she demanded.

Audrey's whimpering stopped. She held the charcoal between her fingers, but otherwise didn't move. Putting her hand over Audrey's, Clara pressed the charcoal down to the paper.

"Easy does it, Clara," Mr. Arbutnot said quietly.

"Draw it," Clara urged. "Draw what you see."

Audrey's hand began to move, slowly at first, and then with quick, stuttering movements. She gazed straight ahead, not at the paper, drawing blindly from memory. Mr. Arbutnot rose to stand beside Clara and watch the picture gradually take shape. It was a drawing of a tree. Not the great elm tree in Washington Square Park, but a smaller, slender tree that appeared to be right below a window—Audrey's own window, Clara guessed, because the drawing included Pish Posh's front stoop, with its short flight of brick stairs. Snagged on one of the slender branches of the tree was a necklace.

"Whose necklace is that?" Mr. Arbutnot asked.

"Mine," Audrey said. "It's mine." Clara had never in her life heard such sadness in a person's voice.

"Is that the diamond necklace, Theodosia?" Mr. Arbutnot asked gently. "The one you thought Frank Ploy had stolen?"

"Yes."

"But how did it wind up in the tree?"

Audrey was silent for a moment, her brow furrowed in recollection. "It must have been the night of the party," she began hesitantly. "I had leaned out the window to watch Mr. Ploy walk down the street. The necklace's clasp must have come undone and fallen onto the tree branch."

Suddenly, Audrey jumped up and leaned out the window. Mr. Arbutnot held her back by her elbows as if he were afraid she might fling herself out the window.

"It's a mistake!" Audrey screamed out the window. "Please! Oh, please, you must let him go!"

Clara looked out the window now, too, and saw that beneath the ancient elm, the little portrait artist looked up, trying to find the source of the shouting.

Audrey shook her head and began to cry. "It's too late," she said, her voice breaking. "He's swinging from the noose now. His legs are still kicking . . . oh, I can't bear it!" Audrey stopped. She pulled her head back in and slumped down in the rocker. "That's all, that's all."

She fell silent, and for a moment no one spoke.

"Theodosia," Mr. Arbutnot said gently, "as I count to ten you will slowly drift up to the lake's surface. You will be sitting in your bedroom in the year 2006, and you will be Audrey, who makes soups at Pish Posh. One . . . two . . ."

When he reached the count of ten, Audrey took a deep breath and looked around.

"Is it over?" she asked.

"Yes, it's over."

"Did I say anything useful?"

"Perhaps," Mr. Arbutnot replied lightly. And he sat back down and recounted to her what she had told them, none of which she remembered. Audrey listened, and when he came to the end of the story, she turned to look out the window at Washington Square Park, shaking her head in wonder.

"But how could I have survived this long? How is it possible?"

"I don't *know*. But I have a suspicion." He leaned forward, his elbows on his knees, and he paused to gather his words before he spoke. "Occasionally, when a person goes through a traumatic experience, a portion of that person will split off, detach itself from the situation so that they can avoid the pain. It's usually temporary. But your case is very unusual. It seems that you split off completely. You went one way, and Theodosia Pender went another way. You became two different people. But here's the problem. You're not a *whole* person . . ." He searched for a way to explain it, and suddenly bent forward and pulled off a splinter of wood that jutted out from the edge of the rocking chair.

"This splinter, for example. It's made of the same stuff as the rest of the chair—same molecules, same atoms. Look, it even has the black paint along one side of it, like the paint on the chair. When it's attached to the chair, it shares the chair's strength and abilities: it can hold a person's weight, it can rock back and forth. But when it splinters off from the chair—as you have from Theodosia—it can't function in the same way. It still exists, but it is very much weakened. I think, Audrey, that's what has happened to you."

"Then what can be done?" she asked.

Mr. Arbutnot nodded, expecting the question. "Well, it's only a guess, but I'm thinking that we have to find some way to reattach that splinter to Theodosia."

"But Theodosia is long dead by now," Audrey objected.

"She may have had children, grandchildren, great-grandchildren, and so on. Her descendants would be a part of her, too."

"But how on earth would we find them?" Audrey asked.

"Oh," Clara piped up confidently, "that won't be a problem."

CHAPTER EIGHTEEN

"Good afternoon, *Hither & Thither*." The receptionist answered the phone on the first ring.

"I would like to speak to Ms. Mandy, who writes the Ask Ms. Mandy column, please," Clara said. She had gone home and was sitting in her living room, eating a tuna-fish sandwich cut into four perfect triangles.

"Get in line, honey," the receptionist said dryly. "Half of New York wants to speak with Ms. Mandy."

"This is Clara Frankofile." She waited a second for this information to have its intended effect.

"Really? No kidding? *The* Frankofile, of Pish Posh? Hang on a sec, honey, I'll put you right through."

Clara took a bite of her sandwich while she waited. In another minute, a man's gravelly voice came on the line.

"S'up?" he said.

"I'm trying to reach Ms. Mandy, of the Ask Ms. Mandy column."

"Speaking."

"You're Ms. Mandy?"

"Only in the column, sweetheart. Now, what do you want, and make it quick. I'm investigating some joker who claims he's the freakin' long-lost brother of the crown prince of Spain. Looks like he actually owns a deli on Long Island. Now, who are you, and what's the question?"

"I am Clara Frankofile and I need you to trace someone's descendants." There was a marked pause at the other end of the line.

"Frankofile, huh? This the daughter of *Pierre* Frankofile?" Ms. Mandy said her father's name with a kind of sarcastic sneer, which she found offensive.

"Yes, he's my father," she replied briskly. "Now, here is my question: I would like to know the descendants of a woman who lived in New York City until 1812. Her name was Theodosia Pender."

"Yep, yep, Theodosia Pender, sure. And your phone number . . . yep, yep, got it . . ." She could hear Ms. Mandy typing information into a computer. "You know, I don't usually do this for people on demand," he said. "Most people have to write in and wait their turn. But I'll do this for you on account of your father. Me and your dad go way back, kid. We were childhood friends, back in the old neighborhood."

"You're from France, too?" Clara asked incredulously. The man had absolutely no trace of a French accent.

"France? Are you kidding?! In Brooklyn, sweetheart. Good old Avenue U and Seventh Street. He grew up one house down from me. And his name was Marvin Bumf, not Pierre Frankofile. We used to flip burgers together at the local diner when we were teenagers. Matter of fact, you could say

I owe my career to your father. A few years ago I ran into some of our old buddies in Brooklyn, and they told me how Marvin Bumf had changed his name to Pierre Frankofile, and that he was saying he was some rich guy from France. It was then I got to thinking that maybe there were lots of other characters running around New York who were big phonies, too—no offense, kid. And bang! Ask Ms. Mandy was born! Anyhoo, I'll check out this information for you and call you back. Good to talk to you, kid. And tell your dad Larry Broccoli—that's me, doll—says, 'Nice goin', Marvin! Your secret is safe with me, pal!' "

Clara hung up the phone, blinked down at the sandwich in her hand, then put it back on the plate. Marvin Bumf? From Brooklyn? It was impossible . . . and yet, now she remembered something.

She got up and went to the Neighborhood in Brooklyn Room. She flipped on the light and waited while the Brooklyn morning began to dawn. As the room grew brighter, she saw what she was looking for: the street sign said AVENUE U and 7TH STREET. The same street that Larry Broccoli had mentioned on the phone. The street on which her father had grown up.

It suddenly occurred to Clara that she had never wondered if her parents were Somebodies or Nobodies. The question had never crossed her mind. What if her own parents were Nobodies? The thought was so alarming that she immediately tried to decide which they were—Somebodies or Nobodies—in the same way that she decided about everyone else, through clues and logic and gut instinct. But no matter how hard she tried, she just couldn't decide. It was as if she had a blind spot when it came to them. They were simply her parents. And for that moment she caught a glimpse of what life must be like for most people, who walked around not knowing how to judge anybody.

Then, quite suddenly, she realized the most extraordinary thing: I am Clara Bumf. *I am a Nobody.*

The thought literally made her legs buckle, and she had to hold on to the signpost to keep from falling. She felt like a tight ball of string that had been suddenly and violently unraveled. There was nothing left of her but loose ends and insubstantial bits and pieces.

The smell of pizza and the shouts of Brooklyn children were too much to bear. She left the room and shut the door firmly. Then she went to her bedroom, crawled into her bed, and pulled the covers all the way up to her nose.

For a full twenty minutes, she stared up at the ceiling and thought, I am the most pathetic human being on this planet. I am the most pathetic human being on this planet. I am the most— And she would have gone on for hours more if the phone by her bed hadn't rung. She didn't answer it. But she did stop thinking long enough to listen to the gruff male voice on her answering machine.

"Hey. You there? No? Well, this is Ms. Mandy. I found the answer to your question. Yoohoo . . . you there? Going once . . . going twice . . ."

Clara picked up the phone.

"I'm here," she said.

"Boy, you sound crummy. What, did your hamster just die?"

"Yes."

"Oh, boy. Me and my big mouth. I'm sorry, kid. Okay, so, here's the story. Theodosia Pender moved up to Rochester, New York, in 1812, and got married to some old, rich dude a few months later. She had one son. He wasn't too healthy, apparently, but he lived long enough to get married and have a few kids of his own. As a matter of fact, all of Theodosia's descendants were pretty sickly types—it's amazing that there are any of them left today. And there *ain't* many. Actually, there's just one. Her name is Fiona Babbish, and she's the end of Theodosia's line. No husband, no kids—"

"Fiona Babbish! I know her!" Clara cried. She was the young, frail-looking heiress who came to Pish Posh every night, alone, to eat her bowl of soup.

"Well, she's your gal. Best of luck, kid! And condolences about the hamster."

CHAPTER NINETEEN

The Pish Posh restaurant was busy as usual that evening. Clara sat at her little round table in the back. She did not have the waiter bring her a tuna-fish sandwich—she was far too agitated to eat—but she did take periodic sips from her tomato juice as she watched the front door.

She had seriously debated whether or not to go to Pish Posh at all. Now that she knew she was Clara Bumf, the daughter of a burger flipper from Brooklyn, she felt like one of those phonies Ms. Mandy investigated. And her parents were phonies, too, bigger phonies even than she was, because they had lied about themselves all these years.

In the end, however, Clara put on simple black dress #103 and her black sunglasses—which now seemed like merely a silly costume, meant for Clara Frankofile, not for Clara Bumf—and went to Pish Posh.

"Feeling better?" her mother asked when she walked in.

"Much," she muttered. Under her breath, she angrily added, "Lila Bumf."

Seated at her table, Clara looked around at all the fabulous, glittery customers. They were chitter-chattering and laughing, and they all looked glowingly confident in the fact that they were, indeed, Somebodies. And hard as she tried, Clara could not detect a single customer who was becoming a Nobody. Not one. She examined what they were eating, and she checked their shoes for scuff marks and their fingernails for bite marks. But she found nothing. She wondered if she were losing her ability to detect a Nobody from a Somebody. It was an unnerving sensation, like pawing around in an unfamiliar, darkened room.

Finally, at half past seven, Fiona Babbish walked in, her shoulders slightly slumped as usual. She sat at her table, and Lila did not bother to put a menu down for her. She always ordered the same thing—a bowl of the daily soup.

Clara stood. Everyone in the restaurant turned to watch her as she headed for Fiona Babbish's table.

"Looks like Fiona is getting the boot," Prim LeDander said to Bitsey. Both were wearing belts with SASSY LADY printed across them.

"My eyebrows itch!" Bitsey complained as she rubbed at the stubble over her eyes, where her eyebrows were growing back.

"Stop that! You'll give yourself a rash," Prim said severely, and she scratched a little at her own eyebrow stubble when Bitsey wasn't looking.

When Clara reached Fiona's table, Fiona turned her gaunt, colorless face up to her and said, "Oh, dear, you're going to ask me to leave, aren't you? May I finish my soup first?"

Clara signaled to the busboy to fetch a chair, which he did, and she sat down opposite Fiona.

"Ooh," Ms. Babbish moaned mournfully, staring down at her soup as if she were about to say one last fond farewell to it.

"Ms. Babbish, I'm not going to throw you out," Clara assured her. "I'm coming to you with an idea."

"Oh . . . must I make a decision of some sort? I'm not very good at that. It always makes me feel a bit light-headed." And in fact, poor Fiona Babbish had already begun to turn even paler. Clara thought about what Ms. Mandy had said, that all of Theodosia's descendants were very sickly and frail.

"Ms. Babbish." Clara lifted her glasses and propped them up on her head, then leaned across the table confidentially. "What do you think of the soup at Pish Posh?"

"The soup?" Her expression perked up immediately, and Clara noticed for the first time that she was actually quite pretty. And did she imagine it, or was there a small bit of Audrey in her eyes and the set of her cheekbones? "Oh, the soup is divine!"

"How would you like it if the person who makes the soup at Pish Posh became your own personal live-in chef? She could make soup for you every day—breakfast, lunch, and dinner. Any soup you wanted. What do you say to that, Ms. Babbish?"

"Well, that would be . . . oh, certainly it would be . . . I would have to meet her, of course . . ."

"Of course," Clara agreed. "Stay put. I'll be right back." Clara got up and rushed into the kitchen. Pierre was whipping a pan of mushrooms across the flames on the stove and simultaneously screaming, "If you burn that fish, I will pull out all your molars, string them up, and use them as a door chime! Ah, Clara, *chéri!*"

She ignored her father, whose use of French now infuriated her, and marched through the kitchen to the back, where Audrey was ladling soup into bowls that were lined up by the stove. Clara went behind the serving counter, snatched the ladle out of Audrey's hand, and put it down on the stovetop. "Come with me."

"I can't," Audrey protested. "I'm in the middle of—"

"I've found her," Clara interrupted. "Theodosia's great-great-great-great-great-granddaughter. She's right outside, in the dining room."

"Are you sure?" Audrey looked at Clara in disbelief.

"Absolutely sure."

Audrey wiped her hands hastily on a rag and rushed out from behind the counter, blindly bumping into the busboy, before Clara grabbed her elbow and guided her through the kitchen.

"What do you think you're doing, you *petite cochon*, you nearsighted little pig!" Pierre bellowed at Audrey. "Keep serving that soup, you *grande* nitwit, or I will—"

"I have a message for you, Papa." Without letting go of Audrey, Clara stopped right in front of her father and faced him squarely, looking right into his pink, damp face. "Larry Broccoli wanted me to tell you this: 'Nice goin', Marvin!' "

Pierre Frankofile blinked twice. For the first time in twenty years he was at a loss for words, an occurrence so extraordinary that the entire kitchen went silent—the dishes stopped clattering, the waiters stopped shouting their orders. Even the pans seemed to stop sizzling.

"Let's go." Clara's grip tightened on Audrey's elbow, and she led her out the kitchen doors and into the dining room.

The customers had never seen a cook in the dining room before, and they stared aghast at her soup-splattered apron. Up front, Lila looked as if she thought her daughter had gone completely mad, and dashed back to the kitchen to consult with her husband (who was not much help, because he had shut himself up in the kitchen pantry, where he was sweating profusely and rocking back and forth on a twenty-five-pound sack of rice).

At Fiona Babbish's table, Clara pushed Audrey forward and said, "Audrey, meet Fiona Babbish."

Audrey carefully smoothed her white cook's jacket, then shook Fiona's bony hand. The two women looked at each other for a moment. Fiona Babbish seemed to be assessing Audrey in her own quiet way. And Audrey, for her part, was looking at Fiona with an expression that can only be described as grandmotherly. For even though the two women looked to be about the same age, Audrey was, in a way, Fiona's great-great-great-great-great-grandmother.

"You're very pale," Audrey said to Fiona.

"I haven't been well for some time," Fiona admitted.

"A little sun would do you good," Audrey told her. "And perhaps an occasional walk. To bring some blood to your cheeks."

"I do enjoy a leisurely walk," Fiona agreed.

"A *brisk* walk," Audrey admonished.

Ms. Babbish cleared her throat and gave a quick nod to Clara. Apparently, she had made up her mind. "I would like her to be my live-in chef," she said to Clara. "Yes, I would like that immensely."

Clara grinned at Audrey, waiting to see her reaction. But to her surprise, Audrey was not smiling at all. In fact, her brow was cinched in a deep frown.

"Thank you. That's very kind. But I'm afraid that would be impossible," Audrey demurred.

"I don't see why." Fiona's voice grew a little peevish. "I have everything you could want—a well-appointed kitchen, ten extra bedrooms—you can take your pick. I would pay you a generous salary, of course."

"It's not that," Audrey said. "It's . . . I have a view in my room that I am very attached to—"

"But there are other views to look at," Ms. Babbish said simply.

Audrey looked at Clara for a moment. Then she nodded. "Yes. Yes, I suppose there are."

CHAPTER TWENTY

One week later, Clara and Annabelle were spending the entire day in Clara's apartment, going from room to room, because Annabelle was determined to see them all. Consequently, they took a hot-air balloon ride (just to the ceiling, but still . . .); slammed into each other with bumper cars; bobbed in the ocean waves; visited the life-size gingerbread house, where they chewed the armrests off a Gummi sofa and licked all the chocolate doorknobs; sledded down a snowy hill, at the bottom of which they pelted each other with snowballs; ate wads of cotton candy at the state fair; and rode the roller coaster (Clara screamed so loud that Annabelle had to plug her ears). Finally, when they went skating on a frozen pond, Annabelle broke out into hoarse, loud laughter.

"What's so funny?" Clara stopped skating and put her hands on her hips. They were both wearing the Skating-on-a-Frozen-Pond-Room costume, which was a powder-blue parka and a yellow knitted hat topped with a giant pom-pom.

"You keep whistling," Annabelle cried.

"I do not."

"Yes, you do. Every time you go around a corner, you whistle. Go ahead. Start skating and see for yourself."

So Clara started skating again and found that it was true: every time she turned a corner, she flung her arms out to the side and started whistling. Then she remembered that Dr. Piff had told her she used to whistle while she skated.

"I think it helps me keep my balance," she said.

"You are a strange duck, Clara."

They went to every last room, until they had reached the absolute end of the hallway. Then, for old times' sake, they scaled the climbing tree, racing each other to the top.

The girls perched on the tree's highest limbs and looked down over the city. The day was bright and warm, but with an occasional breeze that whipped their hair and cooled their necks. Uptown the streets were set in a strict and regular grid, like a checkerboard. But downtown the streets squeezed together into a chaotic tangle as the island of Manhattan grew narrower and narrower, like a spidery maze of streams, with cars and people flowing this way and that, as though they were each propelled by their own currents.

"I canceled my membership in the American Association of Burglars, Crooks, and Ne'er-Do-Wells," Annabelle said out of the blue.

"Are you really going to quit burgling then?"

"Well, my dad says it's not the burgling that I love. He says I'm addicted to danger."

Clara glanced over at her and noted that Annabelle was sitting on the slenderest branch possible and swinging her legs back and forth nonchalantly.

162

"He might be right," Clara said.

"Yeah, he might be. He promised to sign me up for rock-climbing classes on the weekends. And I figure I'll take another stab at school. I guess it won't kill me. I'm going back to the Huxley Academy. And if I hate it . . . well, let's just say I'm not throwing away my Spyfocals anytime soon." She turned suddenly to look at Clara and said, "Hey, whatever happened with that envelope I stole for you?"

It was then that Clara finally told Annabelle the entire strange tale of Audrey Aster, from her first encounter with Ms. Blurt all the way to Fiona Babbish. Annabelle listened without saying a single word, and Clara began to wonder if Annabelle thought she was simply making it all up.

"So," Annabelle said when Clara was finished, "it was old Ms. Blurt who ratted me out and gave my address to you, huh? Well, she never liked me much anyway. In her art class I liked to draw all my faces with giant nostrils—it drove her mad!"

"You believe me then?" Clara asked.

"Heck, Joan of Arc comes to our house every Tuesday! Why *wouldn't* I believe you?"

"But another strange thing happened just last night," Clara said. "Fiona Babbish came into Pish Posh again. I hadn't seen her since Audrey went to work for her. She came in alone, as usual, sat down, and ordered some soup. So I went up to her table and asked how Audrey was doing.

"'She's gone,' Fiona said.

"'Do you mean she quit?' I asked. But Fiona shook her head. She said that Audrey had left one day without a word.

But that her glasses and her sketch pad were still in her room. She said it was as though Audrey had simply vanished off the face of the earth."

"Cripes, that's weird," Annabelle said. "Was Fiona angry?"

Clara shook her head. "Not at all. In fact, she seemed kind of cheerful. Plus, she looked a whole lot healthier. She had color in her face, and her shoulders weren't all scrunched up. You know what I think?"

Annabelle shook her head.

"I think the splinter's been reattached," Clara said.

A gusty breeze made the leaves riffle, and one of the bigger ones detached from the tree and sailed down, past the terraces, and finally landed on top of a bus, where it was whisked away.

"Hey, you know what we should do?" Annabelle said. "We should go down to the Huxley Academy and let old Ms. Blurt know what happened. Besides, I want to tell her that I'll be back in her art class this year. That'll send her over the edge! Serves her right for ratting on me."

On their way to the Huxley Academy, they cut through Washington Square Park. It was teeming with people—jugglers, musicians, skateboarders, dog walkers. By the fountain a man with purple hair and pierced eyebrows was swallowing a flaming torch.

The little artist who had once offered to sketch Clara's portrait was at his usual spot under the ancient elm tree—the

Hanging Tree—and when he saw her, he patted the chair beside him energetically and called, "Sit, young lady. I will sketch your portrait. Only ten dollars. Sit."

Annabelle hooked her arm through Clara's and whispered, "Ignore him."

"Wait," Clara said. She stopped and stared up at the tree for a moment, spotting the thickest limb, the one Frank Ploy had been hanged from. It was hard to imagine that the tree once had such a gruesome history. Now it simply gave shade to the little artist and whoever sat for their portrait, its splendid canopy of leaves nudged by the breeze, high above their heads.

The artist smiled at her encouragingly and patted the chair again. After a moment's hesitation, Clara pulled away from Annabelle.

"Sure, why not," she said, and she took a seat.

"Don't let him charge you a penny more than it's worth," Annabelle warned. "I'll be right over there if you need me, watching the fire-eater."

"Okay, but don't get any ideas," Clara called after her.

The little artist sharpened his pencil with a penknife in quick, expert strokes, and then flipped his sketchbook to a fresh page.

"Now," he said, pencil poised above the sketch pad, "how do you want to look? Shall I make you look glamorous? Sophisticated? Shall I make you look like a movie star?" He swept his hand toward his sketches of movie stars.

"No," said Clara. She removed her sunglasses, folded

them up, and put them on her lap. "Just make me look like a kid, please."

While the little artist's pencil whooshed across his sketch pad, Clara sat perfectly still beneath the shade of the Hanging Tree—no fidgeting, no hair twisting, no smiling. But she did tap her feet twice on the ground, and then once more for Dr. Piff, just to let him know she was thinking of him.